Marked

A Collection of Erotic Tales

MARKED

A Temptation Press Anthology

Marked

A Collection of Erotic Tales

A Temptation Press Anthology

UNION LAKE, MICHIGAN

TEMPTATION
PRESS

Acknowledgments

Temptation Press would like to thank all those that contributed to this anthology. We chose to showcase five new voices that best embodied our vision for this anthology.

We would also like to thank all those on our Temptation Press team for all their hard work and dedication to these projects.

Contents

Bird Call

January Wren

Clarence Pemberton adored his wife. It was a truth that he knew well, one that he kept buried in his heart. He watched from the window as Grace wandered their famed garden, a place where every sun-loving flower blossomed, and a heavenly scent filled the air. It was a far cry from the crowds and the hate of life in London. Both of them were keen to reside at his family estate. There, they had only the company of each other and the servants that gathered near. His grandmother had moved to a dowager cottage, though she frequently came to see them when she wasn't staying with his sister and her family.

The weather had always favored the gardens. The trees provided shelter when it rained, and the soil was filled with nutrients, as the gardeners often commented. There were fields of brilliant color, where petals never seemed to fall, and every visitor's heart fluttered. It was a place of love and wonder, making the famed wild gardens witnesses to more than one marriage proposal.

When his brother-in-law Francis had proposed to Kitty, he hadn't made it past the front steps of the estate, Clarence remembered with a wry smile. They had wanted a crowd, though later, society would hear of how Francis had proposed to her privately beneath the great oak tree and promised to make her will his for as long as they lived. Instead, their weekend party had seen Francis drop to one knee and were enchanted by Kitty's shimmering tears. They were like diamonds, their grandmother, Lady Emma, had crowed, and made sure to record it as so in her diary, one that they were meant to publish for the sake of posterity a decade after her death. Clarence himself knew how poisoned his grandmother's pen was, and thought that society would never be prepared to receive it.

It hadn't been long before the entire town had known, and Clarence knew that his sister's calling card was still full over two years later. Only instead of potential suitors, her card was filled with every mother in London, who wished for their own daughters to learn from her. Kitty's beauty was often celebrated, and more than one poet dedicated his poetry to her. Clarence and his sister favored the Fitzgerald side of the family, their eyes dark, and mouths dancing with humor. His hair was a quiet shade of red, while hers was brighter, the same as their personalities often were. His sister wanted to hold the world in her hands while he wanted to make his life his own.

With their grandmother's agreement, Kitty had worked to lure Francis and his many country estates into matrimony, a game that Clarence watched with amusement. Kitty had known what she wanted and had chased Francis with unrelenting abandon until the boy had faltered, and willingly decided to break countless heiresses' hearts. It was Kitty that Francis wanted, or no one at all, he'd written in a letter which both Clarence's grandmother and his sister had delighted over.

She would make a terrifying matriarch of society, Clarence freely admitted, if only to himself and his pigeon, Aster. The bird often listened to him as Clarence chatted away while handling his correspondence and issues related to the estate. Grace was the one to find the bird, rushing into his study only a few months ago.

"I found a bird in the gardens! He's hurt, Clarence, oh, please!" She'd come closer to than she'd ever had, close enough for him to touch. He'd kept his hands still, resolutely holding on to his quill. "Will you help me catch him?"

The word *yes* had sprung from his very tongue before his thoughts had caught up to him. They fled to the gardens, where Clarence scooped the bird up and held him against his chest. The bird had ruined his jacket and pulled at his ear with his sharp beak, but Grace had been enchanted with him.

"May we call him Aster?" she asked, and his name was set.

The bird was a terror, as pretty as he was, and set the servants on edge. Clarence found that his study was the only place that Aster liked to rest, aside from his forays into the garden with Grace. The thought to set Aster free had never occurred to Clarence, not after the bird had settled right into his cage, weeks after his wing had been healed. Grace often cooed when she saw him and cuddled him near, leaving Clarence to wonder what it would be like if she wanted *him* so near, as she once had.

If he was honest, as he often was, Clarence knew that he would have never said no to her. Grace hadn't even asked him whether she could keep the bird; instead, she had graced him with her smile and held his hand tightly in hers when he admitted that Aster had grown rather fond of his place in the study. She was like the sun, her flames leaping and rolling beneath his skin, making his chest ache for her.

"He's a part of the family now," Clarence had said about Aster, and Grace hadn't let go of his hand. It was one of the few times she had willingly touched him.

He had never forced her, no. The thought of it turned his stomach, the feeling as intense as it was on their wedding night. When she had undressed before him, and he saw the scars painted across her skin, he had made a fool of himself. Tears had dripped down his cheeks, ugly, filthy little things that formed an endless river between them. She had fled from the room while he had hobbled after her until the pain in his leg had seized him too badly to continue after her.

They slept in separate rooms. His was one that he had never wanted to use. There were times when he rested against the door to her bedroom and wondered and waited for childish things. It was the same as when he was a child, one born with a twisted leg, and thought that he could race down the hill. He had spread his arms wide and wanted to fly, his heart hammering inside his chest as he made himself move. He passed twelve steps before he found himself bruised and crying out in pain, his leg limp beneath him. It never followed his will; instead, it imposed its own upon him. His grandmother had servants trail in his wake as if he were a horse meant to be broken. He wasn't meant to be alone, she said, and he knew that she spoke truly.

He often cursed when he felt his muscles bunch, and his nerves twisted beneath the skin as if his leg had the right to make his very life its own. He was subject to its wills and its feelings, terrible wracks of pain keeping him abed for days. Was he not a man, the same as any other? No, Clarence admitted, as he rested his temple against the glass pane. He was not the same as other men, men who were free to chase after the women they loved. He could not parade with her in ballrooms, nor hold her tight against his frame as they galloped on horseback through the glistening fields. His wife was never made subject to his wills, nor was he, in turn, bound to her whims. It was the falter of his walk that stood between them, the pain in his leg that never went away.

He made words his companions before Grace ever came, as he spent countless hours in the manor's library, and learned the classics by rote. He learned how sentences could please and how authors could make their readers wonder. He wrote letters to Grace during their courtship. The ache in his wrist was one that he welcomed far more than the pain that frequently kept him abed for days. He wanted to give her something more, as ink splashed across the page, and promises lined the words that he laid down.

He longed to sweep his wife off her slipper-clad feet and crush her against him while her laughter teased his ear. He had wanted her the moment he saw her after she accompanied her mother for tea with his grandmother. He had been a young man then, and she was younger still, as he listened to the tittering whispers of his grandmother and her guests. It was only toward the end of their tea that he appeared, and he found himself enchanted by the stain painted across Grace's cheeks and the way that her hand fluttered to her chest. She was the prettiest girl that he had ever seen, including his sister, who never longed for society to call upon her.

When Clarence was younger, he had never worried about hastening to have heirs, fully aware that his sister would have a plentiful marriage. It was only with Grace that he dared to dream of a little girl, one with her dark hair and his dimples, or a son who would have his height and her gentle nature. It was a dream that he wished to make his reality, the estate itself longing for children to fill it. They would have a dreamlike childhood, one that would fill the halls with laughter and the pitter-patter of tiny feet. Clarence smiled despite himself. *If only.*

He wished and he wanted for their match to happen, though as a grown man, he knew that a betrothal required far more than that. It was an earthly matter, their match depending far less on Heaven, and more on his grandmother's skill at negotiation, and the sizeable inheritance behind him. Grace would want for nothing with him, a truth that was stressed to her family and Grace herself.

Clarence came to know her as they took gentle walks in the park, with her mischievous sister trailing behind them. Lydia often raised her voice, making biting comments about others that milled around them, yet he knew how to laugh at the best of her antics.

"She is the same as our dear Kitty, I fear," he noted, and Grace had knowingly laughed at that, both of them used to being the one their family forgot. There was little need for them to be remembered, as dutiful and polite as they were.

"There is nothing for us out there," Clarence had whispered the first time that he had dared to draw her trembling hand into his own. No one had been aware as they slipped away from the grandest ball his grandmother had ever thrown, one that celebrated the news of their engagement. He had never known what it was like to want before he was with Grace, the childish kisses that he'd once shared with a servant's daughter leaving him with little to compare. "But there is everything for us here."

She was the same as the sweetest of does, with her dark eyes open wide, and her lips parted. She was the most wonderful of sins as they kissed, and their tongues hungrily sought one another. There was a fire in his chest as he held her close against him. She stepped on his toes, wanting to be closer to him still.

"Please," Grace mewled, and he was lost for her, as he always knew that he would be.

"My darling girl," he'd murmured as he made her his own.

For it was there in the small closet that he taunted and teased her. She tugged her gown past her chest, and he brushed kisses across her skin, from the curve of her nose to her trembling chin, and down further, to her bare collarbone. He heard her gasp when he nipped at her breast, his teeth lightly skimming her nipple. He wanted everything from her, a truth that she felt keenly as his erection had jutted against her hip.

Gods be praised, his leg had not faltered then, not as he sank to his knees and felt her hands tangled in his dark hair. He wanted to know every thought that crossed through her, the same as he wanted to know the sounds that he could draw from her. Her body was one that he wanted to know the same as he knew his own, just as he opened himself to her in turn.

"Let me taste you," he begged, and she had blushed further before moaning her agreement.

It was a tangible sin between them, one that would bind them to one another; they were each other's first and only. It was this that Clarence wanted, more than he had wanted anything before, even more than the nightly prayers that he'd cried as he begged God to make him the same as any other man. His leg was his foil, and yet, in her arms, he'd felt nothing toward it. His resentment, his anger, his sheer sorrow was washed away in the sheer marvel of her embrace.

"I'll give you the world, my lovely girl," he'd said before he buried his face in her cunt without shame.

His arms had wrapped around her thighs as he began to lap at her folds, his tongue gliding between them. There was a slick muskiness to her that he reveled in. His nose bumped against her clit as he worked his tongue deeper inside her. She moaned his name, a sound that he knew he would remember for the entirety of his life with her. *Mine, mine, mine …*

He had heard that men were ruled by their cocks and had never understood, nor would he, Clarence thought, as he found that she had him by his soul; his heart and his lungs were held inside her fist as she rocked her hips against him. It was more than his body that he wanted to be tied with her, more than his cock, and more than the need for her that unfurled beneath his skin. He wanted to be used for her pleasure. Her cries spurred him forward as he drove his tongue inside her. He wanted to imprint her taste on his tongue as he swallowed the juices that she spilled into his mouth, an offering that he wanted all of.

❧

"Grace," he longed to cry, as he found himself unbearably hard at the memory of it all. Clarence gasped as he snaked his hand down his trousers, and faltered at the urge to take himself in hand.

It was something he rarely did since she had fled from him, their disastrous wedding night paining him intensely. Yet his memory of pleasuring Grace was one that he wanted to relive again and again, even if she never allowed him to know her again.

"You're so lovely," he said as his hand curled the base of his cock. His hands were calloused, whereas hers were soft and uncertain. Clarence remembered how sweetly she had once stroked his worried brow. She was kinder than the saints were in the stories, and he wanted, even then, to swath her in pure gold. "More lovely than you'll ever bloody know."

His hips bucked as he began to stroke himself, jerking his hand up and down his throbbing cock. His eyes were half-open as he watched her in the garden, and he made a pained noise at the thought of her seeing him. He wanted to pleasure her again, his mouth aching at the thought of suckling at her breast while his fingers dove into her cunt. She was all that he wanted, as pretty as any nymph in her flowy gowns and with flowers wound through her hair. Surely, they could overcome the gulf between them.

His knees weakened as he felt himself teetering toward the edge, and he tipped his head back. She was all that he could see. He admired the elegant show of her neck and the way that she skimmed her hand across the shrubbery. He wanted the estate to be her home as much as he thought of it as their own. He often set books aside from the library that he thought she would enjoy, and found himself gathering flowers by hand that he knew she admired. He would give them to the servants afterward, asking them to fill her rooms with them. It was more than her body that he wanted, as he missed their quiet chatter and the sheer intimacy that had arisen between them before their wedding night. She was his friend, his confidante, and his wife, someone more than he could have ever dared to dream of.

Oh, how he dreamed of her. He dreamt that he buried his hands in her hair and had her while she was on her hands and her knees. He often awoke gasping with cum dripping on to his stomach. The memory of her cries was too much for him to bear. At that thought, that traitorous, little thought, he felt his leg buckle, and he cried out as he fell, having little to grab on to.

"Damn it!" Clarence shouted as he crashed to the floor, pain shooting up his leg. It twisted and burned on its own accord, and he gritted his teeth together to keep from crying out once more. It wasn't his desire for a servant to find him a man undone, nor for one of them to tell Grace. No. She couldn't see him as he was, not then. "God, *please*," Clarence said, his hands scrabbling against the wood floor.

Only it was his wife that found him there, as he hadn't the heart to drag himself from the floor. It was the call of sleep that lulled him into believing that she wouldn't see him as he was … until he awoke with her hands cradling his cheeks as she knelt beside him. Her dark hair was undone, and tiny curls drew in toward her cheeks as she gazed down at him. On the other side of the room, Aster was fast asleep in his cage, his delicate wings drawn against him.

"Are you all right?" she asked softly, and he fought the urge to laugh.

He was far from all right, though he found the pain in his leg had lessened to a hum in the background, the needles that pierced his skin less than the nails that came before them. "I'm not, my sweet girl," Clarence admitted, his blue eyes unflinching from her own. He felt shame in his throat, a ball of yarn that he wasn't apt to swallow. "Are you?"

Her thumb drew across his bottom lip, making him wince. He must have bitten it when he fell, he thought. All thoughts came to a halt when his wife pressed her lips against his own. The flame that spread was slow and steady as it crept across his belly. It was far less than the near-painful flame as when they were courting, yet it was true all the same. It was sure instead of swift, and Clarence wanted to clutch Grace near.

Was this how his father felt? It was a question that Clarence had never dared to ask his grandmother. She had assumed hold of their care after they were left with only the servants to care for them. His father wanted only his wife, not the company of his children, no matter how pretty Kitty could sing. Their father had lost himself to feeling itself. He took his mother further and further away from society and her family until they both left the world completely. Their grandmother had only commented on her son once, scornfully noting that he was a man "who felt too much as if he always felt all of his emotions at once." He was a man without control, one that was the same as a beast in the eyes of society.

His sister was nothing like him, apt as she was to twirl beneath the gaze of society and gather its admiration close to her chest. She wanted nothing more than to be its queen and make the others fall beneath her. She was the one who made their grandmother proud, and Clarence freely admitted that he admired, even loved, his sister. Yet it was he who wondered if he took after his father, as if it was a sin passed down to his very soul, and if he, too, would lose himself to feeling itself when it came to Grace. He would lose his soul, Clarence knew, if it meant he could have his wife completely.

"I … I've missed you," Grace whispered, drawing back from him. Only his low whimper stopped her as she stayed inches away from him, her gaze skittering away from his. He forced himself to stay still, knowing that she could easily run from him if she wished. "I-I didn't think you would see them," she admitted, her voice smaller than he had ever heard it. "My scars."

"You knew that I was," Clarence hesitated, searching for the right words. "You know that I *am* a cripple, Grace."

"Mother said." She nodded as if she hadn't known the moment that he first walked with her in the park. They both knew that she had slowed her steps to match his, though she had cheerfully pointed out the pretty birds that she observed and chatted gaily about trivial things as if he were the same as any other suitor … as if he was the same as any other man.

"They're from a time that I never wish to remember," Grace admitted, tears gathering in her eyes. They weren't the shimmering, pretty tears that his sister often shed; instead, the sorrow that streaked down her reddened cheeks was real. His hands moved to cover hers, their fingers interlacing. "When we were young, Mother sought a governess for us, one that would be able to handle Lydia, Edmund, and I. She came with only one reference, but it was from a dear acquaintance of Mother's," Grace hastily added, seeing the raise of his brow.

He knew how close his wife was to her mother still, as she dutifully wrote her multiple times a week. Clarence had never thought to keep his wife apart from her family, as other husbands did. The practice of marriage was as barbaric as its joined partners made it, especially the men that crowed over owning their wives while they drowned themselves in drink. Clarence wanted none of it. He brought their hands near before pressing his lips against her knuckles.

"She never enjoyed our company, nor did we seek out hers," Grace said, her voice slowly gaining strength. She didn't hesitate; instead, she squared her shoulders as she ignored the tears that gathered in her eyes. "Except during our lessons, when we couldn't escape from her. She … she wanted us to listen and to learn." Only their governess's teaching style was one that left his wife littered with scars, ones that mirrored the ones her siblings had. "I was the eldest and wanted to protect them. I *should* have protected them," she corrected herself.

"Grace—"

"No," she interrupted. "I should have, Clarence. I should have told Mother! She had no idea about what was happening, as she was constantly traveling with Father into London …"

It was the same as the shameful rage that Clarence had carried as a child when he dragged his ruined leg behind him as the servants gathered near. However, it was a shameful sorrow, not rage that his wife carried, as she admitted to him. "Our chef at the time saw the governess handing out a punishment, and she was the one who wrote Mother, even after I … I begged her not to." Grace looked at their hands, his so much larger and stronger than her own. "I never confessed to Mother what happened." Her expression crumpled then, the same as parchment dragged across the water. "She pleaded for us to tell her in our own words what occurred, and the others did. But I … I couldn't. I wasn't brave enough to."

He wanted to chase the very words from her lips, though he knew it would do nothing but frighten her. He could picture her well enough, a small, dutiful child that was thrust into the adult world with her siblings behind her. It wasn't right, as so many things in life were, and the taste of copper pooled across his tongue.

"Grace," Clarence began, his tone far gentler than before, "God willing, if we had children, would you expect them to tell you? If their governess was mistreating them?"

"I—"

He squeezed her hand and felt the press of her wedding band. "Do you remember how frightened you were?" he asked, his eyes meeting hers once more. He ached to have her nestle against him, the same as he wanted her to ask him to find the governess and handle the matter for her. He could have a man that his grandmother employed to look into the matter, a man who replaced scruples with a taste for intrigue—and coin.

"I … I was frightened even after Mother let her go." Grace leaned forward, resting her temple against his own. "I thought that she would come back in the night, as she'd promised to never leave us alone. She never tried," Grace hastily added, as if she had grasped his thoughts. "Mother hired a proper governess from

London, one that we all came to adore, and she gave our chef a raise. I … you … *we*," she corrected, "would never allow that to happen to our children. Never," she fervently swore.

"Never," he agreed without doubt. "Nor will I allow another to hurt you, Grace, not even myself."

He was still as she drew her temple against his own, leaving no space between them. "You can't say such impossible things, Clarence," she said, her tone gently chiding him. "Surely you can't prevent everyone—"

"I can."

"Or yourself," she finished before rubbing her nose against his. It was a move that made them both smile as if they were children in truth once again.

He felt the fire roll inside him as it spread into his chest. "Use me if you wish," he said, the words like honey melting across his tongue. "I've missed you, Grace, more than I can say. I—" He closed his eyes then, before opening them once again. "I never wish to see you unhappy, which is something I should have told you on our wedding night. You're beautiful." Clarence swallowed as her face crumpled.

"I shouldn't have run away," Grace said, and he shook his head.

Clarence wanted to be more than a fool when he was with her and knew that the mistake was both of their makings. "I should have found you, no matter how long it took," Clarence countered, "and we should have talked to one another. Truly, my love."

"I … I wish to make things right between us," Grace said with a sudden playful note to her voice. "We never had a wedding night, husband."

It was then that he knew what she intended as she drew her body against his. He felt her flush against him. The pain in his leg was a dull thrum in the background as she nuzzled her cheek against his own.

"May we try again?" she asked.

"For as long as you'd like," Clarence responded, unashamed of how his cheeks reddened. "We will make this right, wife."

Their touches were tender as they began to undress one another; Clarence helped her draw her skirts aside while she tugged his trousers past his thighs. She surprised him by helping him with his shirt.

"I wish to see you," she said, and he knew, once more, that he could deny her nothing.

He was a husk of will, his bones her own as her hands traced the expanse of his chest and the muscles that strained beneath his pale skin. There was adoration in her touch and in his as he drew one hand to her waist and steadied her there. The other held her face in his palm, his thumb caressing her reddened lips, ones that he longed to taste over and over again. Theirs would never be a marriage of convenience, nor high propriety in their rooms.

"I love you."

His words were simple and whispered as he felt her own slick heat draw against his member. He kept his hips still as she began to rock against him, slowly urging him inside her precious place. Her cunt was slick as he slipped inside her, and he heard her gasp as he began to fill her.

"You f-feel incredible," Clarence said, truth behind every word. She was nothing like he had imagined, the feel of her smaller body atop his making her startlingly real. "Don't be a dream," he nearly begged, and she gave him a soft smile, one that made his heart ache. "Please, Grace—"

"I'm n-not," she promised. "I'm real. I'm here with you, Clarence."

He groaned as she moved against him, urging him deeper inside her until he felt the truth of her virginity, as delicate as it was. "Hold on to me," he said, his voice thick.

He never wanted to hurt her but knew that he would. Her eyes scrunched tight, and she stilled against him. There were books in the library that he had once read, describing the act that happened between them, and how they would join fully after her virginity was taken. He knew that his cock was different from his fingers or his tongue, and as he broke through her hymen, she cried out in shock.

"I've got you," he said, feeling lacing every word. "I'm here, my love."

She felt as if she were made for him, the entirety of his shaft gliding through her slick walls. It was nothing like before when he had taken himself in hand, a crude imitation of what their pleasure could be together. She tipped her head back, baring her neck to him, and moaned his name aloud. She held his heart and was his home, he thought, understanding it more than he ever had before. She was the only home that he would ever know, a home that he never wanted to leave.

The flames engulfed them as he thrust inside her in earnest, his cock sliding in and out of her channel. She leaned her body forward and gripped his shoulders with her hands, her nails digging deep into his skin. He knew that he would wear her marks with pride, his skin unmarred from never knowing war. Sweat rolled down his cheek as he gave the best of himself to her and quickened his thrusts. Her cunt was like a vise around his member, squeezing his shaft as he explored inside of her, yet he couldn't get enough. She whimpered his name as her cheeks flamed. They came as they gasped and writhed against one another with nothing between them but their souls.

"Clarence," Grace gasped, "I-I love you."

"Always?" Clarence begged, and she fervently nodded.

"Always."

They came in tandem, their words twisting about them like silken cords, ones that would never let go. The outer world was lost to them as the moon bathed the gardens in its gentle light, and the stars scattered across the midnight skies. From the great oak tree, an owl called into the night, singing a song of promise and fervent delight.

Heat

Max Carrey

There's a knock on my door, and it bounces off the walls, resounding in my ears. A shiver of uncertainty courses through me, and goosebumps stipple my skin. I toss my laptop to the coffee table, rising from the couch slowly. Who could it be? I know who I *want* it to be.

Another knock, and I jump with anticipation. It has to be *him*. No one else could make me this wound up. I imagine his knuckles rapping on the door, his fiery, burnt-sienna eyes, and the way they so firmly latch onto me as if he's undressing me with them while also stripping my mind of inhibitions. I always feel so vulnerable with him, so open, so easily enflamed. I lick my lips, wishing I could taste him on them. I dash to the door on tiptoe, moving silently. My hand outstretches to unlock the door, but I retract it, hesitant.

"You there, Bri?"

I screw up my face in torment. Then I abruptly flick the lock, twist the knob, and open the door. Damien stands out in the hallway. His muscles are tense, and his angular jaw is locked. Those reddish-brown eyes disrobe me completely.

"My friends say you're no good for me," I say with a shaky voice, drinking in the flicker of hurt that splashes across his striking features.

His brow pinches. He works his jaw and grinds his teeth, then suddenly, his jaw goes slack. "They're right; I'm bad for you," he replies with a dangerous edge.

I inhale sharply, my chest heaving. The air is icy, and my eyes dance around his skin, visualizing the warmth of our bodies together. I exhale jaggedly. It's a burning ache I can't ignore. I lunge at him, and Damien instinctually moves into me, wrapping his arms around my waist. I smother his lips with mine, and they're softer and more tender than I remember. Tasting a sweet singe of heat, I trace his mouth with my tongue. As I breathe him in, a woody, oaken scent bristles my nerves, electrifying me.

I press my fingertips into the nape of his neck, pulling him in closer. Taking several tottering steps, he follows me into my apartment, closing the door behind him. His arms keep me upright as my feet slip against the floor, but I can't break from him. I have to have him further. I trail kisses across his jawline and playfully take his earlobe into my mouth, sucking at the tender flesh. He growls, sending vibrations running through me. I sigh as I go to kiss behind his ear, but suddenly, he goes rigid. His shoulders square off, his hold on me tightens, and he pulls back.

His eyes search mine. "You can do absolutely anything to me," he whispers. "Just not that."

My hands loosen around his neck, a stray finger edging behind his ear where his mark is. He twitches, so I let my finger drop, though my eyes catch it. The mark is in the shape of a blazing flame. It's not a usual tattoo. Its hue shifts, almost catching the light, unstably changing from orange to red, then to a fiery yellow, and I swear I can see the sparks pop and explode within it.

"Why? It's as if you're ashamed of it."

He casts his head downward, resting his forehead against mine. When he speaks, his voice is deep, the tones pulsating within each other. "It's complicated."

"It's beautiful," I say, whispering as if it's a secret.

He draws his face back up to pierce me with those eyes. His warm, golden hair shaggily hangs down to tantalize me.

I wrap my fingers around his hair and gently pull it off his face. "You're beautiful."

His lips split into a grin, and he smothers me in it, decorating me in kisses. His arms tense, and he suddenly hikes me up. My legs naturally wrap around his hips. The impulse urgently overtakes me as I feel the heat rise and burn in my cheeks. I let loose a giggle that causes his grin to twist into a satisfied smirk. I bite my bottom lip, and I feel him shiver around me. One hand is draped across my back, holding me at the waist, while the other trails down my backside. Reaching around, he finds my warmth under my dress. I melt into his embrace, reeling in desire. I can feel his virility, feel it rise, yet his focus is still only on me as he traces lazy circles. His movements are sensitive, but also flaming in heat. His fingertips send sparks inside me, kindling a fire in my belly. I moan, and his grip on me tightens while his brow pinches closer together. His muscles are stiff and strained, yet he goes to touch me further, ignoring his own needs.

"Stop," I tell him, barely able to voice it.

He listens immediately, watching me carefully.

My breath hitches, ecstasy begging me to not wait, but I crave all of him. "I want *you*."

He moves his hands, and I writhe under him. His eyebrow arches devilishly as he leans into me, sucking against the tender spot on my neck he'd discovered the last time. He's toying with me, bringing me to the brink, and my aching for him intensifies. I grab a fistful of his hair and yank his head back, and he chuckles tantalizingly. I can't take it anymore. I yearn for him.

Reaching down, I find the buttons and zipper to his jeans. I rip them off and push my panties to the side. I take him in my hand, guiding him, and he thrusts. I cry out, and an ecstatic smile stretches across my face. I can feel my longing swell as I rhythmically move atop him. Our shallow breaths grow more ragged as our breathing quickens. My eyes try to close and lose myself in it, but I force them to stay open. I won't lose sight of him. The light streaking in between the blinds is a haze of fading light that sparkles against the flaming mark. His fingertips, his whole entire being, his *essence* fills me up with warmth. The movements become shuddering, the pace undulating. Suddenly, waves crash over me, and I scream in pleasure. Damien spasms, his muscles pulling taut as a guttural moan escapes through his parted lips.

"I don't think you're so bad for me. You can't be. Not when you feel so good," I groan, and it transforms into a satisfied giggle.

Shame etches his face as he looks down upon his body in disgrace. "I am, though … I'm so sorry, Brit." He settles me gently onto my feet.

My knees are wobbly, but I swat his hand away angrily despite having to grasp hold of the wall for support. I collect myself and furiously adjust my dress. My gaze narrows irately as I watch him fix himself as if trying to be rid of all traces of me. I burst out suddenly, "No! How dare you say something like that to me after what we just did?"

His eyes flare in surprise as he flexes his aching fingers.

"You can't tell me *that* was just sex. I know you can feel it too …"

Damien casts his eyes away from me, and they lose their heat, freezing over. "I'm sorry I—"

"You just can't, right?" I interject, knowing all too well what he was going to say because I've heard it before. "Why are you running? You're running from me, from your feelings, from yourself, and why? For what?"

"I don't ..." He hesitates, his voice breaking off. His mouth goes to close, but I startle him.

"No! You don't have the right to decide things for me. Tell me what's going on," I plead.

His gaze wavers, but stays steadfast. "I don't want to hurt you."

I shake my head, confusion riddling my brain. "You already have."

"I—"

"I know you're sorry! I know, okay?" I stop, trying to swallow the lump in my throat and keep the tears from falling. "You make me feel cheap. You come and go, saying you can't get me out of your head. You touch me and make me love you—" My voice hitches.

Shock paints his face, then his eyelids flicker as if trying to fight something back.

"I deserve an answer," I mumble, stepping up close to him. I temper my anger and grasp hold of his forearm delicately, and I can feel him sink into it. "You hide so much of yourself. Tell me."

His Adam's apple lurches in his throat, and I can feel a slight tremor coursing through his veins. He nods his head. "Okay."

"Really?"

"You're right. You deserve to decide for yourself." He looks behind us toward the living room and adds, "Perhaps you should sit down."

"What are you going to tell me? That there's been a death in the family?" I say sarcastically.

Damien rolls his eyes and huffs, "Oh, come on." He takes me by the wrist and leads me to the couch.

I sit down next to him, wrapping my hands up in his. I give them a squeeze to reassure him as I see the fear warping his face into worry. "Out with it."

"My father …" His voice dies out.

"Your father?" I urge.

"… is Hades, ruler of the underworld."

My grip on him loosens as I become lightheaded. The room begins to tilt. *He's insane.* "Um, I—"

"I know what you're thinking, but let me prove it to you." He scrunches his face, pinching it together in concentration. He shakes rigidly as veins start to pop out of his skin.

I don't realize that I'm holding my breath until my lungs start screaming at me. I gulp in air, but I choke on it, sputtering out ragged coughs. There is no reasonable explanation for what I see. His veins are literal fire. The sight explodes in my mind, freezing it up in the spectacular awe of it. An orange, reddish-yellow heat courses through his veins, making visible the intricate network, and it's as if I can see through him. A burning glow gleams off the side of Damien's head as he relaxes his face, melting into the sensation. I try to peek at the source of the glow; he notices and turns his head to the side to provide me a clear view. His mark is alight as if it actually burns.

"You really *are* beautiful," I mumble as my mind swims in staggering confusion and wonder.

He laughs as he turns back to me, and I note how even his eyes have lit up with heat. "It's the mark of the demigods."

"Ha!" I exclaim loudly and then tear my hands from his to cover up my mouth, trying to keep the shock from spilling out. Suddenly, my hands feel as if they have been pricked with icy needles. My skin feels so frosty in comparison to when his hands were wrapped up in mine, and I realize he quite literally generates a fiery heat. "You're made of fire," I say, my words tumbling out of me.

He chuckles. "Only partially." He raises a finger, and a flame erupts.

My jaw goes slack, and my eyes transfix upon it hypnotically until he folds it back into his palm, smothering it. I shake myself out of the trance and try to will my mind to focus. "So you really are the son of … Hades?"

"In true Greek god fashion, Hades had a night with a human, my mother, and then she had me. Each demigod has a mark that represents his or her blessing. I was blessed with the fire of the underworld." He shakes out his shoulders, and the glowing light dims until it has completely faded away. His veins recede, and their burning color calms back to his pale skin tone. "I didn't expect to—" His face twists up as he cuts himself off. "I don't want to put you in danger. Some creatures would look to hurt you to get to me. I tried to make myself quit you, and it was weak of me to come back here and put you in danger."

"Stop," I whisper. I reach out my hand and settle it across his jaw. My fingers trail up into his hair and continue to his mark.

He slumps, leaning his head into my palm, his eyes closed as if to imprint my touch into his memory.

"I don't want you to keep leaving … I want you to stay."

His eyes shoot open, and the corner of his mouth twitches as if begging to smile. "I don't want you to get hurt."

"I only hurt if I'm not with you," I reply, blinking rapidly to keep the sudden tears in my eyes from falling. I can see his jaw tense, and his fingers flex. "Why did you come back? Tell me the truth, not what you think you have to say to protect me."

"I …" he begins.

I bite down on the inside of my cheek. My arm wavers, but my fingertips grasp hold of him tighter. My heart is thudding madly against my ribs, and I can feel it breaking loose. It's teetering, about to fall, when finally, he parts his lips to speak.

"I love you."

I draw him in. He lets me guide him, and I place a gentle kiss on his lips. I'm so much more aware of the warming tingle that courses from him into me. This time, I'm the one to pull away, leaving my forehead pressed against his. I sigh before whispering, "Come what may. I want you. I want you to stay with me."

"Are you sure?"

"You better not keep asking, expecting me to change my mind, because I won't."

He finally succumbs into a smile. "Then I'll stay."

"Yeah?"

"Yeah," he confirms, pressing into me with his lips and sending sparks to envelop me.

He's fast asleep beside me, but I'm just too excited to relax. Perhaps it's the realization that Damien is a demigod, which breaks down everything I thought I knew of the world, or maybe it's the fact that he's finally here to stay. I'm encased in his arms, cradled in warmth, and I can feel his chest rise and fall with each breath. I can't seem to scrub the smile off my face, and I delicately trace his fingertips with my own, as if I need reminding that he's real.

My floors creak, and my eyes flick to the shadows in the corners of my room. A black pit of darkness swells inside it. My smile drops as panic jerks me upright. I shake Damien awake with my trembling hand. "There's someone here!"

He jolts up groggily just as a voice emerges from the darkness.

"Aren't you two just so cute?" The lights flick on, and a towering figure with a wry expression chuckles. "There, that's better."

"Ares," Damien growls. Stomping to the foot of the bed, he tucks me away behind him. "What are you doing here?"

I peer around him to see the intruder, and the sight of him sends jitters through me. I had always thought of Damien as quite large with his brawny muscles and tall height, but this man is a beast. He makes Damien appear small and scrawny. His eyes are sharp like daggers, and a greedy, severe grin pushes up a ravaged face full of scars and burns. Every inch of him is rippled, taut muscle, making even his skin look like armor.

"Just observing," he answers coyly. He cocks his head to the side and narrows his eyes to scrutinize me. I can tell he's taking note of my hands wrapped around Damien's waist and the rigidity of his stance; it deepens Ares's grin. "She's quite pretty for a *mortal*, but then again, you'd find that charming, wouldn't you? You're half of one yourself." He curls his lip in disgust and rolls his massive shoulders back, letting the bones yawn and crack.

Damien shoves me further behind him, and I begin to tremble as the name rattles around my brain, igniting recognition … Ares, the god of war. I try to keep my teeth from chattering as I uncontrollably shake, my nerves frying with fear.

"Leave," Damien snarls. "You are nothing but trouble."

"Now is that any way to talk to a god?"

I can't see his face, but I know Ares is no longer amused. I can picture his roguish expression sliding off into agitation, for a dangerous edge overtakes his voice. My fingers push into Damien's stomach, and I can feel him tense against me. I can sense his worry, and it frightens me.

"You incite war and violence wherever you go. You murdered Poseidon's son, and you would try to take the throne at Mount Olympus if you could, or perhaps even the seat of Hades. You are not wanted here, so I will tell you once more. Leave." I can hear that Damien's words are said through gritted teeth, and I see him plant his feet to the floor more steadily. He's preparing himself for something. My stomach lurches, and I feel sick.

Ares cackles sinisterly and throws out a hardened boulder of a fist, but Damien grapples it with both hands. He struggles to hurl him off. Shaking against Ares's immeasurable strength, a battle cry rumbles from Damien's throat. Ares's other hand suddenly seizes

Damien's neck, taking him off guard. He wheezes painfully, and his face turns blue as he is slowly raised off the floor.

I scream, "No!" Snatching my lamp from the side table, I rush forward and smash it against Ares. Shards of porcelain stick into his skin as larger chunks clatter to the floor. Anger flares in his eyes, and blood trickles down his snarling face. It's enough to distract him. His hold on Damien loosens, and Damien takes advantage of the opportunity by bringing down his forearm on Ares. Buckling over, Ares lets him go, and Damien rushes to my side, shoving me behind him again.

"Be gone with you!" he shouts, clenching his whole body. The mark behind his ear flares to life, burning. His veins pop from his skin, coursing with fire, a smoldering red. He raises a splayed hand, sparks flying off his fingertips. Suddenly, the sparks erupt into flame. The flame swirls throughout the air, licking and lashing out until forming the shape of a hound. The hound's paws singe the floor as it charges Ares before sinking flaming teeth into his heel.

Ares cries out, swiping at the creature, but his fist does nothing to the emblazoned hound. Ash flakes off into the air, and char coats my nostrils. His body is being swallowed up in flame as the hound runs circles around him, leaving walls of fire in his wake. Turning his bloodshot eyes toward Damien, Ares growls, "Your father will hear about this!"

"I'm planning on it," Damien replies coolly. Just as the flames completely surround Ares, Damien curls his fingers into his palm, snuffing the fire out. Nothing but burn marks and piles of ash are on the floor. Ares is nowhere to be seen.

"Where'd he go?" I ask, blundering out from behind Damien.

Damien's fire has subsided, and his posture relaxes. Heaving, he slumps to the bed as he runs his hand over his glistening brow. "I sent him to the underworld."

I clamber over to him on my shaky feet and kneel down before him. He's put his face in his hands, his body bent over in torment.

My heart quickens its pace again, worry coursing through me in stinging anxiety. "Are you okay? Are you hurt?"

"No, I'm fine," he says, his voice heavy with guilt. "But you could have been killed."

"You too," I remind him. Finding his chin, I gently push it up to reveal his face. His eyes are watery and are losing some of their heat.

"This is what I was afraid of."

"So?" I say casually, my nerves beginning to calm.

"*So?*" He shakes his head and stares at me as if I'm delirious. "This is dangerous. You could die because of me."

"I'm probably still more likely to die from a car accident or choking on a cracker," I sarcastically reply through a wicked grin, though my smile seems to do the opposite of my intentions.

He grabs me by the shoulders and stares at me intently, his gaze melting me. He wets his lips and says softly, "Don't ever joke about something like that … I don't ever want to lose you."

"Then keep me close," I say, tracing a finger around his parted lips. I run my thumb up his cheekbone and swipe away a tear. "If you don't want to lose me, then don't ever let me go."

He lunges forward and clutches me desperately. As he kisses me, I can feel warmth radiate off him in more vibrancy and passion than ever before. I tremble as it prickles my skin in an icy-hot desire. He pulls back from my lips and whispers into them, "I love you."

⁂

I awaken to the sun burning through the blinds. I shoot out a hand and find that I'm alone in bed, and the sheets are all messily scrunched. Damien is clattering around in the kitchen. I blink the fog out of my eyes, yawning and stretching my limbs. The time on the clock reads 12:52 p.m. After the whole ordeal with Ares, Damien promised to hold me until I fell asleep. I was still rattled by the intrusion, though I think it was as much a comfort for him as it was for me. It seems I've slept in while he has been up cleaning, I see. The floors are shined to a polish, and barely any sign of last night's inferno is noticeable. The air is even light and ash-free.

I stagger out of bed, still sleepy, and find Damien huddled over, putting away cleaners under the kitchen sink. "You didn't have to do that," I remark, yawning again.

"It was my mess, and I should be the one to clean it up." He suddenly jumps up and whips around. Grabbing hold of me, he hurls me onto the counter.

I let out a shriek and slap him playfully across the shoulder. I dangle my legs, letting them kick into the cabinets lazily. His face beams so much brighter today, his worry lines smoothed out across his chiseled features.

A smile flares up, and he exhales, muttering into my ear, "I never did thank you for saving me."

"What?" I laugh. "When did I save you?"

"You smashed a lamp over Ares's head." He chuckles as if recalling the memory. "Sorry about your lamp, by the way."

I giggle, my cheeks flushing with heat. "You're welcome. You know, you might be a demigod, but I'm a ninja."

"Oh, really? I didn't know ninjas were in the habit of using lamps as weapons."

My face screws up cockily. "That's because you're an unskilled, untrained, handsome brute."

His fingers squirm over my body, tickling me, and I fold into myself. I break into a fit of giggles until he stops, and he relaxes into a more serious tone. I can see the adoration in his sienna eyes. His hand weaves into my hair. "What are you thinking about?" he asks curiously.

I bite my bottom lip. "Why don't I just show you?"

I draw him near and plant a kiss upon his mark. This time, he doesn't pull away. This time, I can feel his body heave with aching.

He hungrily lurches forward, swiping away everything on the counter to clear it. I nervously laugh with anticipation as I help to pull him onto the counter. I lie back against the cool slab, and suddenly, he's above me, tearing at my clothes. My insides flutter. No one has ever wanted me so badly. Still, he hesitates once he has me lying naked. Then he abruptly laughs.

"Really? Now is *not* the time," I joke, knowing that he's not really laughing at me because I could see the faraway look in his eye.

"No, no, you're beautiful … I was just thinking that we might break the counter."

"Well, I'm up for redecorating," I say humorously, now tearing at his clothes until he's naked too.

He leans forward and sends kisses down my neck. I run my hands over him, over his arms and down his back, but my hands slip upward as he lowers himself while trailing kisses across my skin, sucking and licking at my flesh. I inhale and exhale jaggedly once he moves across my breasts, before leaving a hand there to grasp and tug in tantalizing movements. His tongue goes lower down, looping over my belly button, and then coming back up to take my bottom lip into his mouth. I moan, pushing my body against him further as one of his fingers finds my warmth. My toes curl, and my fingers latch around him. I can feel him stiffen, though he ignores it, as once again, his focus is on me. This time, I let it be because I'm drinking in the moment, and he's showing me his patience. Nothing is hurried, because we both know *this* is where we're meant to be, and *who* we're meant to be with.

Second Skin

Wolfgang Domino

Two blocks from my office in Manhattan sat a little bar called Lankey's. College kids mostly ransacked the place, buying Pabst Blue Ribbon a dollar a pint. Eager law school students from CUNY, the City University of New York, crowded the place during the weekends, singing karaoke and pounding shots of fireball. Lines of cars parked around the block and people stood on the outside smoking cigarettes, huddling in close together to combat the dropping temperature. Patter from their conversations hit my ears as I passed through the crowd, but they hadn't been talking about anything juicy enough to eavesdrop.

The volume of the place hit me in the face like a boxer as I slid inside. Once, when I first moved to New York, I stepped foot in Lankey's for some takeout. The wings were black and hard, and the fries were chewy and soft. That had convinced me not to come back until I got a mysterious call. In the back of the building, someone with a mic butchered a Led Zeppelin song. The thick crowd at the bar made passing through difficult. Everywhere I looked, I expected to see her. She'd called me and said it was urgent. My eyes searched every face in the crowd, but I couldn't spot her.

"Over here." I heard a voice just a beat above the screeching at the microphone.

Wrapped tight in a grey hoodie hiding her face, Ana sat in a booth. Her finger tapped against the table. As I sat down, she didn't even look up. "I'm sorry about the anonymous call in the middle of the night. I didn't know who else to turn to."

"Are you okay?" I asked.

With her eyes still focused on the floor, she avoided the question. Sitting across the table from me sat one of the most popular women in New York. She was not a celebrity, but she'd been dating a man named Michael Manavati, who'd just entered the biggest trial in the city.

"You do know this is a bar full of law students, right?" I'd known that from the day I ordered the food. A man sitting at the bar told me all about the nearby campus and the regulars.

"No, I didn't know that. I'm not from around here," Ana said, sliding further into her seat.

Ana Dean and I had a history, long before she'd taken up residence with Manavati, who'd been the second in command for the most significant Mafia family in the city, perhaps on the entire east coast. During medical school, we'd dated. Ever since the first time I saw her face on the front page of a paper, I'd tried my best to avoid her and the trial, but like all things at that level, I couldn't. Her face had been pushed into my face several times over the last few months, leaving me no way to escape her picture or the heartache that came with it. From what I gathered, she testified against him, digging up all kinds of dirt after finding out he had another girlfriend.

"How can I help?" I asked.

"You're a plastic surgeon, right?"

I couldn't deny it. Ana knew I'd been on that path back then, and it wouldn't take much of a guess to determine I'd probably graduated and moved onto my career by now.

"That's right."

"I need you to redo my face."

A long pause fell between us as I thought about the consequences. Helping Ana meant probably getting myself in some trouble too. Her ex had a lot of connections, ones I didn't want to cross. He probably had someone looking for her.

"I would like to help, but ..."

"Are you going to help me?" Ana asked, looking over her shoulder. "I've got a target on my back, and I can't trust the witness protection program. He knows people on the force. He's gotten addresses of people before."

A lot of things crossed my mind as I stared at her. I didn't want to go through with it because of the face she already had. She had such a natural, beautiful face. It wouldn't look as good when I finished, but I also understood the situation. She didn't have many options.

"You're such a pretty girl, Ana. Is that really what you want to do?"

During medical school, I'd chosen plastic surgery, and she'd chosen pediatrics. We went steady together for a while before she told me she didn't want to be in New York anymore. We broke up, and she dropped out of school. Rumors came back to me that she'd never left and got caught up with the wrong crowd.

The horrendous portrayal of the Led Zeppelin song ended, and people clapped. I was appalled that people would clap at that. Another person came over the mic, threatening to do a Metallica song. I wanted to grab my coat and run for the door before they ruined my favorite band for me.

Ana picked at her fingernails as she stared down at the table. I couldn't see her face from the depths of the hood, but I would have bet she'd been sorry for some of her choices. "I don't have a choice, Simon. I need to do something. Right now, I'm a sitting duck."

As she said this, she looked around the bar, waiting for the men to bust through the door.

"Is the trial over?"

"Yes. I already testified."

I'd never imagined we'd be sitting in a rundown bar talking about remaking her entire face. I took in her looks for a second, remembering why we'd dated in the first place. She was of Latin origin and Mexican descent. She had beautiful, black, straight hair and a wonderful complexion. Even though she'd broken my heart, I couldn't help feeling bad for her. Nobody deserves to have their life threatened as she did. Nobody. I couldn't imagine having someone after me like that. It almost didn't feel real.

"Fine. I will do it. It's not going to be easy, but we can figure something out."

She perked up in her seat, eyes bulging from her skull, and a beautiful smile crossed her face. I remembered why I'd fallen in love with her in the first place, and I feared it could happen again. She could take my heart easily if she so chose to do so.

"You need a place to stay?" I asked, looking around the bar, her paranoia playing on me.

A waitress approached, and I waved her off. I didn't want her to see Ana's face, not as dangerous as things were. I didn't want any connection between Ana, myself, and this bar.

"Are you sure?" she asked, an edge of excitement in her voice. "That would be great."

We got into my black Mercedes and drove through the city, careful to make sure nobody had trailed us. It felt surreal, or almost like a dream, to have her in my life again. It also felt dreamlike because someone was after her. As we drove through the city, Ana told me the whole story. She told me about Manavati cheating on her and all the crimes he'd committed. He'd sold drugs, killed people, and bribed people. As she ran through his criminal roster, she told me about how she'd been surprised when they got him because he'd known connected people. He thought he'd become untouchable.

"You wouldn't have believed the ego on that prick," she said.

As we walked through the door of my apartment, Ana's eyes got big. She looked around at all of my décors. As her sneakers tapped across the tile, she looked straight ahead at the painting. It wasn't a painting per se but a replica of Salvador Dali's painting *The Burning Giraffe*.

"This is a nice place," she said. She walked through the apartment, looking at the various art. She'd known about my fascination with paintings and that I'd minored in art history. "Did you ever get around to painting your masterpiece?"

"No. I gave up painting shortly after college," I said, but it wasn't right. I'd given up painting after Ana left and never picked it up again.

"That's unfortunate," she said, walking further into the apartment. "Your career must be going well."

"Yeah, I took up a private practice. I share an office with a couple of other doctors. We do all right."

The door to the balcony was off the kitchen. Ana stopped there, drew back the curtains, and gasped. "That's a great view," she said. The door whooshed open, and she stepped outside into the brisk fall air.

"Yeah, it sure is."

Lights twinkled and flickered on the skyline, looking like rhinestone jewelry. Her hands clasped the rails as she stared out onto the majestic view. "You've done well for yourself, Doctor." She chuckled. At the bar, she'd been a nervous wreck. Now, she seemed relaxed. She looked as if she could breathe again. Her shoulders relaxed, and she even smiled on occasion. She stood out there, staring for a bit as I walked inside the kitchen.

"Are you hungry?" I asked, looking through the pantry at my options.

"Starving," she said.

"I could whip us up some pasta."

"You always were a talented chef."

A memory of cooking for her came back to me. We'd been in our dorms, working hard on a project, and we'd both gotten hungry. I whipped something up, quick and straightforward. She'd said it was the best thing she'd had in days. Back then, we both lived on a budget, so we ate a lot of processed foods, but I'd wanted to make her something special.

"Would you like some wine?" I asked.

"Red, if you have it," she said. A conversation we'd had in college came to mind. She'd said something about white wine tasting like vinegar, and that she preferred red. "I'd drink toilet bowl cleaner if it would help me forget the past few weeks," she said.

The laugh burst out of me like a cannonball. "That bad, huh?"

"You have no idea. I had to stand in front of all those people in court and tell them all the horrendous shit he'd done. All the while, I thought he'd tell them about the money."

The wine sloshed out of the bottle, and I looked up at her in surprise. "Money?"

She took the glass from my hand, drank from it, and smiled. "Oh, yeah. I didn't just break up with Michael and testify. I robbed him. I didn't exactly get the chance to count it, but it's a lot."

The strong scent of spaghetti sauce filled the room as we reacquainted ourselves and relaxed in the haze of alcohol. Everything felt as it had before. It's strange how we can fall back into those old habits. We remembered inside jokes long since forgotten. It was like we picked it up right where we'd left off.

As we sat together under the fluorescent lights, I couldn't help thinking about the money. Ana only touched on it, but I wanted to know the whole story. I didn't dare ask her all the details because

I didn't know what she'd do, but I thought she might run away. How much did Ana take? Where had she hidden it?

"You never married?" she asked, pouring us another glass of Cab.

"Nope. You were the last serious relationship I had. I dated another girl a couple of years ago, but we weren't compatible, and it ended quickly."

After dinner, we sat out on the patio, staring down at the city below. The lights glimmered and dazzled. Sometimes, when I felt down, I'd spend a night sitting out there, staring at the city. We sat close together on my porch swing.

"Do you remember how hopeful we were in medical school?" she asked. "We were going to take the world by storm. You, me, our friend Tony ..."

"At least Tony did," I joked.

"What happened?"

"Doctors Without Borders. He's gone to Africa, Asia, and a few other places. We video chat sometimes," I said.

Something in her eyes said she wanted me. She looked at me with yearning. Ana slid in closer, and the floodgates opened, full of old feelings. I'd been in love with her then, and now, I could still remember the taste of that love. I wrapped an arm around her and held her close as I had all those years ago.

We kissed a familiar, wet kiss. Ana's tongue slid into my mouth, and I couldn't stop the passion from boiling over. Things escalated as I kissed back and gripped her breast in my hand. Everything felt familiar but yet brand new. The bra worked as a shield, blocking me from getting a good feel. It didn't stop me from enjoying what I did feel, like a teenager in the basement at a party.

"I've missed you," she said, breathless from kissing. "I've missed you a lot." Her lips clasped with mine again for another round.

Many floors above the bustling city, Ana's hand slid down my leg. No woman had touched me in a long time, and I missed the feeling of a woman. Vigorous kisses passed up and down her neck, each earning a deeper moan. After taking a break from her neck, I nibbled on her earlobe. That worked like magic.

The hoodie disappeared in a matter of seconds, as did her shirt. Even though the air outside felt cold, we both powered through. All we needed to warm up was each other. Snapping off her bra didn't take much effort, and it, too, fell to the wayside. She had marvelous boobs, untouched by a surgeon. I took her perfect pink nipples into my mouth.

Between my legs, I could feel the monster awakening. The throbbing of my penis trapped between my leg and pants ached, but I wouldn't have changed it. I suckled on Ana's breasts as she looked down at me in the throes of passion. While my mouth worked her breast, my hand wandered. I started at the top of her waist and worked my way down, taking my time, raising bumps on her flesh. The denim of her pants resisted my touch.

"Take me," she whispered, raising the hair on the back of my neck.

Before I could do anything further, she lifted herself from my lap and unsnapped my button. Ana bent down on her knees and took me in her mouth. Her lips graciously slid up and down my shaft as my toes curled, and my brain filled with euphoria. I tried to contain myself. Every muscle in my body tensed and eased. My head rolled. I closed my eyes, feeling the motion.

She stroked it for a while, teasing the tip with her tongue. It came to a point when I had to stop her. If I didn't stop her, it would be over in a matter of seconds. I took a second, my chest heaving, and stared out at the city. I regained my composure and lifted her from her knees, kissing her deeply before switching places.

Before sitting down, we unsnapped the button to her jeans and pried them from her legs. Her panties came off next, finding a home on the floor with the rest of our laundry.

"Oh, the seat's cold," she said as she sat her bare ass on the metal swing.

My tongue taunted her clit. I kissed, sucked, and batted it around, trying my best to make her scream. I hadn't made love to a woman in a long time, and I wanted to impress. My tongue slid between her lips, thrusting deep inside. I sucked, licked, and lashed. Ana's head leaned back, staring up at the stars, and she clasped a hand over her mouth.

As I ate her out, her legs twitched and spasmed next to me. I had to hold her still just to keep my position. Her moans and screams were muffled behind her hand. Twice, she'd nearly closed her legs with my head between them. I moved up to the little man in the boat, sliding a finger inside her. With a rhythmic motion, I slid my finger in and out while caressing her clit with my tongue. She curled her toes and squirmed, sliding up the seat like she was trying to escape me. I loved the sound her wet pussy made while I penetrated it with my finger.

"Oh, Simon," she moaned, taking my chin in her hand and kissing me.

My dick couldn't get a fraction harder without exploding. We switched places again. This time, my bare ass took the metal seat, and she climbed on top. We kissed as she rode me. Her hips swayed in sync with an inaudible beat. As she rode me, I took her breasts in my mouth again. I bit and sucked and squeezed them.

Up and down, she hammered on top, doing nothing to cover her mouth from moans of pleasure. For a few seconds, I'd grown concerned about my neighbors but then decided that if they didn't like the noise, they could fuck themselves.

"I'm almost there," she said into my ear. Her hands clasped the back of the swing, and she slammed into me hard and fast, trying to get off. "Fuck, fuck. Oh, my God," she screamed before coming to an immediate halt.

After we finished, we took our time dressing. Being in public had always been a fantasy of mine, and I guessed an empty balcony many floors over the city would have to work. We'd had a lot of fun.

"Wow. You brought your A-game," she said.

In the orgasmic aftermath, we sat in the stillness of the night. Over the rail, the city continued to twinkle below.

"It's so peaceful up here," she said.

That night, we lay in each other's arms, making pillow talk, and working our way to sleep. Her hand swept up and down my torso, dabbling with my chest hair at times. It felt good being in her arms again—too good. Part of me thought the shoe would drop at any moment. There were mobsters out there looking for her, after all.

The following morning, Ana made us breakfast. The smell of bacon and sausage awaited me when I walked into the kitchen.

"Oh good, you're up," she said. She put the plate together in a hurry and poured me a cup of coffee. "When do you think we can start on the surgery?"

"We can do the rendering right here on my tablet. It'll be best if we go into the office at night when nobody is there. The last thing we need is rumors about mysterious people coming and going."

"Two creams, one sugar, just like you like." She placed the cup in front of me and kissed the top of my head.

"That's an impeccable memory," I said.

The TV blared on the counter, showing pictures of her ex. They'd sentenced Manavati to forty years. The news program showed tight pictures of his face as they dropped the conclusion in his lap like a cinderblock. The anchors went back and forth about reduced time, good behavior, chances of parole, and other speculation. I'd expected them to mention Ana, but they didn't.

A smile crossed her face. "I won't shed a tear over that prick."

Commenting on the situation didn't feel right, so I shook my head and waited. We watched the remainder of the program and snapped off the TV.

The program on my tablet seemed to impress Ana to no end. She looked at the graphics and watched as I began to put together her current features. I had a good idea of what I could do with her face and how to contort it so that she didn't lose her characteristics completely.

We went back and forth as we played with the settings on the tablet. We would change the basic shape of Ana's nose or ears and go over it with a fine-tooth comb. Some things we didn't agree upon, but we had an open dialogue about making her look different. We also decided she needed a set of contact lenses. The less she looked like Ana, the better.

After several hours and a few cups of coffee, we came to a conjuring of a woman's face she liked. She stared at it in awe. "That's incredible, isn't it? That we can do things like this?"

"Yeah, it is."

"I won't be answering to Ana any longer. My new identity is Veronica Hernandez."

"Veronica Hernandez," I repeated. It seemed like an honest and straightforward enough name. "I like it. The next thing you should do is make a paper trail. Make sure that you exist according to the government."

She took a long drink from her coffee. "Way ahead of you, Simon. I know a guy who does passports, and he will hook me up. All I need is my new face for the photo."

Going back and forth about how we would fool everyone felt nice. It felt like a scene from a movie. Does anyone get the chance to do something like this in their lives? The action felt real as if the goons were waiting outside the door, and the clock was ticking. We had to get her face changed before they figured out that she lived with me.

We spent the day working on her backstory and purchasing new clothes online. I used my credit card for obvious reasons. If they were even halfway good at tracing people, the first thing they'd do is check cell phones and credit card purchases. When she'd convinced me that she could be another person, I told her I would work on her as often as I could. Such a procedure wouldn't happen overnight, so we planned a few nighttime surgeries.

"We are going to need to sleep. Our schedules are going to get strange for a while," I said.

She followed me inside the bedroom, and we lay down together. I'd set the alarm on my cell to wake me at ten o'clock. By then, everyone would be gone, including the cleaning crew. They usually wrapped up around eight-thirty. I'd made the phone call to the alarm company, letting them know I'd be doing "inventory" throughout the week, and the alarm would arm at strange times.

Ten minutes before the alarm sounded, I awoke with a jolt. I'd had a nightmare they'd come for Ana and tried to kill me in the process. My chest heaved as I sat on the edge of the bed, trying to convince myself none of it was real.

"Are you okay?" she asked, probably awakened by my panting.

"Bad dream, that's all."

Telling her would have resulted in her feeling guilty about our predicament, which I didn't want. I'd chosen to take her in and help her. I could have said no as quickly as I'd said yes, and I didn't want her to reflect on that like I'd made the wrong choice.

We both got up and slid into our clothes. I couldn't stop myself from watching Ana dress. She had an elegance about her when she busied herself. An onlooker would never guess the Mafia had marked her. Nobody would ever suspect the danger she'd brought onto herself. To anyone who passed her on the street, she looked like a sweet girl.

Before allowing her out of the hallway, I stepped outside to ensure nobody was around. I didn't see any suspicious cars sitting on our street or anything like that. With a waving hand, I ushered Ana out of the hall and into my car. She'd tucked herself into the hoodie again.

"Are you ready for this?" I asked, sitting at a red light at an empty intersection. "There isn't any going back."

"I wouldn't want to go back," she said.

I noticed the severity of her tone. I just wanted to know that she'd entertained all of her options before making a decision. If she kept going on as nothing happened, they'd find her and kill her. We had to make her old identity disappear successfully. I'd come up with an idea for that. When the time came, we'd take a long trip up north, Maine perhaps, and dump her purse. Someone would likely come across her credit card and go on a shopping spree. We'd leave a little in her account and let the goons go looking for her up there.

The crescent moon shone brightly over our heads as we drove to my office. At every stoplight, I looked over my shoulder to see if someone followed us. At no point during our trip did I see anyone behind us. The streets were quiet, and I held her hand while I drove. It felt nice to be close to someone again.

The alarm started chirping the second I pulled the door open. I turned quickly to the panel and put in the pin. After we got inside, I made sure to lock the door behind us. The last thing we needed was someone coming up behind us mid-operation.

The strong scent of disinfectant passed through our noses as we walked across the lobby. Everything seemed to be in order. The place always felt eerie to me in the dark. I imagined doctors' offices and prisons to be about the creepiest places when the lights are out. Even cemeteries seemed more welcoming.

Without wasting any time, I got my gear on and immediately began scrubbing my hands. A lot of things crossed my mind as I worked, one of the most critical being that Ana had come back into my life, and I didn't want to see her disappear again. Even with a new face and fake eye color, inside, she'd still be Ana, and I didn't want to let her go.

After the first round of operation, I wrapped her face in gauze, and when she came out of the anesthesia, she babbled about being in love with me. I sat there listening to her drugged confession of guilt for leaving me.

"You're the most wonderful guy ever," she muttered before drifting off.

Under cover of the night, I woke her from the car and rushed her to the front door. I didn't want to bump into anyone on the elevators because they could start rumors. They could tell someone they saw me walking up the hall with a patient. Things could escalate.

❧

It took several weeks, many rounds of operations, and a lot of healing, but things progressed. Not once did she complain about having to go through all the things she did. She even tried her best to remain upbeat. During our negotiation, she'd decided to go up a couple of sizes in breasts too, which I didn't mind.

On the last day, I positioned her in front of the mirror in my bathroom. "Aren't you excited?" I asked.

"Oh, yes! I can't wait to see what I look like." Her eyes gleamed as she clapped her hands.

She'd grown accustomed to looking at the world through the tiny slit in the gauze. Before we pulled off the wrapping, I slid her the contact lenses to ensure the illusion would be complete. An overwhelming feeling of success came over me as we stood there, unwrapping her like a Christmas present. Once the wrap fell on the floor and we both stared at her beautiful new face, I felt like we'd just completed the biggest heist ever. We'd gotten away with changing her identity. People wanted to kill Ana Dean, but nobody knew Veronica Hernandez. If I had to bet, I think she could walk up to her ex-boyfriend, and he wouldn't even recognize her.

She turned from the mirror, looked at me with big eyes, and kissed me. "Thank you so much," she said. "Do you think I'm sexy?"

She didn't wait for an answer. She just continued to stare at herself in the mirror in disbelief. Tears of joy strolled down her face. She spent some time dabbing her eyes, looking at herself in the mirror, and asking me a series of questions. We had a heart to heart. She thanked me for potentially saving her life, and I thanked her for the opportunity. What I didn't say, couldn't say, was that I loved her, and I didn't want her to go.

"What are you going to do now?" I asked.

"Well, I was hoping to stay here in New York and give us a second try. If you're willing, that is."

My heart thumped rapidly. *Ana wants to stay*, I thought with a smile. "That sounds great," I said, taking her in my arms and kissing her.

The skimpy outfit she'd chosen for Veronica's debut wasn't an accident. She'd chosen that intending to seduce me. The skirt stopped above her knees, and the top revealed enough cleavage to make a pastor drool.

"What do you think?" she asked, raising her eyebrows at me.

We walked to the bedroom, where I savagely undressed her, tossing the skirt across the room and revealing those beautiful brown legs. My hand rode up them, sliding into the crevice and feeling her flower with the tips of my fingers. She'd been ready for me.

We kissed, our tongues sliding together like two worms in an intimate dance. With my middle finger, I teased her clit, rubbing it up and down and side to side. She moaned, leaning back in bed and letting loose. Relaxation poured over her as she let me do whatever I wanted.

The face didn't belong to her, but the voice did. The mannerisms did, but the face and the boobs were brand new. Strange thoughts passed through my head as I made love to this woman with a stranger's face. It was exhilarating.

Her top came off next, and I discarded it on the floor. I caressed her boobs as I fingered her until she begged me to go down, which I did. My tongue rolled and played in the folds of her beautiful vagina as she moaned and thrashed on the bed. The nectar tasted sweet, and I couldn't wait to get inside.

"You've been a naughty girl," I said, sliding my pants off.

"That's right," she said.

With a quick jerk of her legs, she slid down the bed, and I entered her. She'd always liked it when I took control. I held her tight, kissing her passionately as I drilled into her as I'd never done it before. As we were in the motion, I could feel her pushing back against me, joining the rhythm. My legs shook below me as I plowed into her.

As things got hot and heavy, I turned her over and entered from the back. I pulled her hair and pounded against her. With each thrust, she got louder, edging me closer and closer to an orgasm. Her voice, those moans, had always done it for me. I couldn't resist the noises she made.

As I drilled as hard as I could, I slapped her ass, hoping it might push her over the edge, and it worked. As soon as I did, she pulled away from me and flopped on the bed.

"Oh, baby, that was amazing," she said. "I take it you like the new look?"

"Oh, yes."

We lay on the satin sheets, naked and vulnerable to each other's touch. We lay there for a long time, not talking, only dancing in the waves of euphoria as they swept over us. It didn't take long before I drifted off.

When I awoke, she walked into the room, and I still barely recognized her. I hadn't gotten used to her new face yet. She smiled at me, and I noticed she had something behind her back.

"What you got there?" I asked.

Veronica pulled a briefcase from behind her back and set it on the bed. She popped the clasps and revealed stacks of cash. "I have to pay you for my surgery," she said, dumping the briefcase upside down. Stacks of cash scattered about the bed.

"That's a lot of money," I said. If I had to guess, I'd say my eyes looked like cartoons. I'd never seen that much money in one sitting, ever.

A wide smile curled up on Veronica's face, and she looked at it with a shrug. "There's a lot more where that came from." She smiled at me, leaned in, and kissed me. "Oh, I almost forgot. I got you something else too."

When she returned, Veronica held an easel and a box filled with painting supplies. She kicked out the legs to the easel and set down the box of painting supplies. Her eyes swept over all the content before she beckoned me to come over.

"This is amazing," I said. I didn't want to tell Ana she'd been my muse and I'd lost interest when she left. "I should paint," I said. "It's been a long time."

Veronica turned her back to me, looked back over her shoulder, and shed her shirt. It fell to the floor. "I'd start pouring that paint if I were you," she teased, unsnapping her bra. She sauntered over to the bed, losing an article of clothing every few feet before lying across the spread in a perfect pose.

Stained by You

Shanjida Nusrath Ali

CHAPTER 1

Tracing the black inked birds on my right wrist, I can't help but shyly smile. The tattoo looks so perfect and beautiful, it's indescribable. Looking up, I meet his deep blue eyes as he smiles back.

"Do you like it?" he asks in his gruff voice.

I nod enthusiastically. "I love it. Thank you so much."

Leaning closer, he cups my face, pressing his forehead against mine.

"Now we have matching tattoos," I whisper, licking my lips.

Love and adoration pools in his eyes as he smiles genuinely, skimming his thumb along my cheek. "Now, about the payment. How would you like to pay?" he asks, grazing my lips.

"Do you accept cash or something else?"

"I'm open to options. We just have this night, Ella."

I nod, ignoring the needle of pain piercing my heart. "Something else it is," I say before our lips touch each other's in a deep, passionate kiss.

⟡

I wake up from the dream with a jolt. Sweat glistens on my neck as my breathing becomes short and shallow. I run my hand through my hair and lick my lips. With my hands trembling, I fill the glass from the bedside table with water and finish the drink in three large gulps. Untying my braid, I loosen some strands of my blonde hair and lean back against the headboard.

Two years. It's been two years since that night, and I still can't get him out of my head. Two years ago, I went to Vegas for a trip with my ex-boyfriend, Logan. Everything was going great until I saw a text from my best friend on his phone saying how much she missed him and how she couldn't wait for him to return back to her. Knowing that he was cheating on me was heartbreaking, but it shattered me to find out that Julia, my best friend, was involved.

Without saying anything or even seeing him, I left the hotel we were staying at and wandered around the city all by myself. I ended up in a bar, planning to drown myself in vodka until I couldn't see straight. My eyes were skimming the menu when I felt someone's eyes on me. It felt so intense that my body shivered. When I looked up, I saw *him*.

I knew where this thing was headed and where it would end, and I was okay with it. But by the end of the night, I wasn't so sure about my decision anymore. He made me feel something different. He made me feel alive … wanton.

Now, here I am, back in New York, living in an apartment all by myself and working from home as a full-time romance writer. That night changed a lot of things in both of our lives. He saved me, but I couldn't save him. He promised me one thing, and one thing only. *I will be back for you. I will be back to mark you, make you mine.*

It's as if I'm stained by him, with no way to remove him from my mind, just like the tattoo he inked on my wrist then. With a sigh, I lie back on my queen-sized bed, covering my body with the blanket. I close my eyes to drift into sleep, trying not to dream about him again.

The next morning, I wake up at my usual time and go jogging in the park. Wearing my sports bra and leggings with my hair tied in a ponytail, I put in my AirPods and listen to the music blasting. After an hour of jogging, I return back home, sweaty and exhausted. I check my mail and skim through the usual bills when a letter catches my attention. I take a seat at my dining table and open the letter and start reading.

Angel,

I promised to come back to you. I promised to mark you and make you mine. The time has finally come. I'm coming soon to get what's mine. I can't wait to see my angel. I can't wait to touch your flawless skin, kiss every inch of your perfect body, and claim you inside out. I want to bind you and take my pleasure from you like a hungry predator. Be prepared to be my prey. We will start with what we left behind that night. I'm coming for you, and when I get out, you better be there.

Love,

Parker

My breathing accelerates, my blood rushing faster and faster. He is coming back to me.

CHAPTER 2

"Drink! Drink! Drink!" the crowd roars as I take shots of vodka one after another to beat him in the drinking race.

My brain is getting foggy and unbalanced, but I don't care. I chug the last shot in a second and throw my hands up, letting out a victorious scream. "Woohoo!" I howl, which I had never done before.

He chuckles beside me, wiping his mouth with the back of his hand as a grin stretches on his lips, making my spine shiver. I literally met him like one ... no, maybe two ... or a few hours ... fuck, I don't even remember. I met him today, and he is affecting me in a way that no one ever has—not even my asshole now ex-boyfriend. He instantly made me forget the betrayal and pain I was in earlier today. Maybe it was because he took pity on me for what I faced, but something in his eyes told me he had other reasons.

"Having fun?" he asks in a husky voice, leaning closer to me as the crowd clears.

"More than ever before." I giggle, and, gathering the courage, I take his hand and drag him on the dance floor with me.

"High Heels" by JoJo booms from the surrounding speakers. Colorful lights shine from everywhere as the people start dancing to the beat. I put my arms around his neck, and our bodies sway together, his hands loosely on my waist. The minute our eyes meet, the tension builds. A zap of electricity spikes between us. His gaze falls on my mouth as I bite my lip and lean closer. He squeezes my waist and whirls me around so that my back is against his front. His leather jacket and black T-shirt tickle my bare back, which is revealed by my red midi dress. His breath tickles my neck. His hands grab my waist, and his hips grind against mine as I feel his hard bulge against my ass. My breath hitches as I throw my head back against his shoulder, grinding against his erection, feeling desire running through my nerves. Being with him feels so different ... so erotic.

"You are so beautiful, my angel. So alluring," he growls at the shell of my ear as goosebumps scatter on my body. "The way you are dancing and moving against me is making every man here aroused. Every man who is looking at you wishes to take my place, but tonight, you belong to me only, don't you?"

I nod my answer as I'm unable to find my voice. I feel tingles between my legs as I press my thighs together. My panties already feel wet from my juices.

His one hand grabs one of my ass cheeks, giving it a squeeze, making my body shudder. "I want to have you so badly, Angel. Do you want this? Do you want me?"

I nod eagerly. "Yes ..." My voice trails off.

His lips sink into my neck. I feel his teeth nibbling my neck and then sucking quickly, soothing the ache. "Let's go," he grunts. He takes my hands and leads me out of the club, away from the noise, away from the crowd, before he pushes me against the wall of a dark alley.

⁂

"Ma'am, we are here." The driver's voice drags me back to reality.

I look outside the window and confirm my destination. After paying the cab fee, I get out and walk toward the guard at the door.

"Yes?" he asks in a stern voice.

Licking my lips, I tighten the hold on my purse as my heart pounds faster and faster. "I'm here to visit a prisoner."

He nods and opens the entrance door before guiding me to another guard behind a glass booth. After I give him the information that he needs, he directs me toward the meeting room. It has several phone booths and a huge glass barrier between the prisoners and the people outside. The ceiling fan keeps the room cool as I take my seat at one of the phone booths and wait.

My eyes cast down, and my fingers lace together. I swallow the lump in my throat, taking deep breaths as I try to control my anxiety. After two years, I will get to see him. Suddenly, I hear a door opening from the other side, followed by the sound of handcuffs and heavy footsteps. When I look up, I see *him*.

His dark-brown eyes bore into mine as he stalks toward me in his orange uniform. He looks different, yet the same. I take in his thick, black hair that tickles that his neck, his pale, olive-toned skin, his plump lips, and his five o'clock shadow. He looks so perfect. A sly grin stretches on his lips as he takes his seat and picks up the phone, nodding at me to follow his motion. I pick up mine, waiting eagerly to hear his voice.

"Angel," he mutters in a deep, heavy voice that makes my thighs clench.

"Parker," I barely whisper.

"I missed my angel. Did you miss me?"

"I missed you so much. I can't describe it in words. Since that night, I've never forgotten about you. After all, you risked your life and future for me." My voice breaks as the ominous memory flashes in front of me.

CHAPTER 3

His lips crash into mine as our tongues tangle together in an erotic dance. His hands curl into my hair as my back presses against the rough wall of the dark alley. I gasp and writhe at his touch. How can he affect me so much? How can his touch make me crave for more and more?

We just met, but it makes me want to know him for eternity. My hands find his arms and give them a gentle squeeze before they wrap around his neck. Growling like a hungry predator, he lifts me up. My legs wrap around his waist while his erection digs into my belly. Oh, God! I want him so badly.

His teeth lightly nibble my bottom lip before his lips descend down my neck, where he kisses and sucks my pulse point. I can hear the distant car horns and people blabbering from somewhere, but none of it matters. Only Parker matters right now, in this moment. His body presses against mine as I feel his right hand lowering down and reaching my panty line, making me gasp.

"I can smell how wet you are from here," he groans.

I whimper, biting my lip, then tug his hair, bringing him closer to me. My hips gyrate against his erection. "I want you so badly," I whisper.

Just seeing that wicked grin on his face makes my whole body ignite in sensation overload. His fingers trace my panty line and go lower until I feel them touching my wet clit, teasing me even more.

"You're wet," he grunts, his eyes on fire as they find mine.

His fingers are fierce as they curl inside the lace between my legs and find my lips. My mouth opens as I part my legs further for him, and I feel my cheeks flush. He is rough. His thumb circles my clit until I gasp, then two fingers plunge deep as I rock for more. I grip on his hair harder, my eyes opening wide as he tugs my head back to feast on the pale skin of my throat. I shiver as he sucks a mouthful of flesh between his teeth and nips hard like he is marking me.

"Ah! Parker," I groan. My hand hooks behind his neck to hold him close, my breathing short and shallow. My nails run down his neck with a primal need to mark him too … to make him mine.

"Do you want me? Do you want my dick inside you? Claiming you … marking you …"

He puts his now-wet fingers into my mouth, and I suck on them, tasting myself. My entire body shivers from his touch, his agitation. I nod my answer and suck his fingers clean. My gaze is honest and desperate as I press against his erection. His fingers, wet with my spit, trail down my throat, reaching the tight neckline of my dress. I arch my back as he takes my weight in his arms like a pro. My nipples are pebbled tight against my dress as he twists them between his fingers through the fabric.

God, I wish we were naked. "Yes. I want you, only you," I moan.

He bites my nipple through the fabric as I throw my head back and moan.

"Please, fuck me!" I breathe, and I hear his own breath hitch.

Our bodies move on instinct, mine yielding without question as I hear his zipper opening and clothes rustling as his boxers drop down. Our gazes fill with need and hunger as I feel my clit aching. In one thrust, his dick is inside me before I can catch my breath. My moan is frayed, and his is deep. He slams are so brutal that my whole body thumps against the bar.

"You feel so fucking tight. So amazing, Angel," he groans, and I push right back at him, wanting rough on top of rough. My ex always was a gentle love maker, which I didn't mind, but this is another level of sensation that I've never experienced in my life—until now.

"More. I want more," I whimper, and he thrusts harder, giving me what I crave.

"Fuck your ex. I want you to be with me. Do you want to be mine?"

I nod frantically as I reply, "Yes. Make me yours … mark me."

"Mine. You are mine only."

I let out a loud cry that is immediately muffled by his hand pressed on my mouth.

"Be quiet. Unless you want to gather an audience."

My pussy clenches tighter with every thrust he makes while he groans against my cheek.

"Fuck. Such a tight pussy."

His hips gyrate harder and harder as I feel his dick making my insides tighten. I want him to be all the way inside me, filling me up more than I'd ever known before. His hand slips from my mouth, and I bite down on my lip to stop myself from crying out, although it is a tough task.

"Yes, Parker, yes! Please!" Sinking deeper, my eyes roll back in pleasure. My pussy starts to pulse faster as I feel myself reaching the peak of my orgasm.

"You are getting closer, aren't you, baby?" he asks, increasing his speed.

I nod, unable to find my voice.

"Come with me. Clench your pussy as you come for me."

"Ah!" I moan louder, resting my forehead against his.

He grunts and growls as his eyes shut tight with his lips parted. His body shivers like mine as I feel him getting closer and closer, his dick swelling inside me.

"Come now, Angel. Come."

His words trigger my body right away, and I latch onto his shoulder, muffling my cries as I feel myself breaking apart. My nerves jitter as I come like I never have before, and for a few seconds, my vision blurs. I feel his dick jerking as he spills inside me with a grunt.

"Fuck ..." His voice fades away.

My legs tighten around his waist as I hold onto him for dear life. After taking a few steady breaths, I feel my nerves calming as I open my eyes and meet his gaze.

His pupils dilate with intensity as he kisses my lips gently, his hand rubbing against my scalp. "Where have you been all my life?" he asks.

I giggle, biting my lip, and leave a peck on his mouth. "Are you mine?"

He nods with a smirk. "We both belong to each other now. I'm stained by you and you by me."

⁂

The memory is still fresh in my mind as I remember the night that he claimed me as his. The night he became mine. The night both our lives changed forever.

"How are you?" I press my palm against the glass barrier, but he doesn't return my touch, making my heart ache. Does he hate me? Does he resent the night we met?

"Don't, Angel. I don't hate you," he answers through the phone as if he can read my mind.

"You should. You are here because of me ... your hands cuffed ... all my fault." My voice trembles as I feel tears emerging in my eyes.

"No. Never blame yourself for it. You and I both know it was either him or you," he says with a sneer. His jaw clenches as if he is being taken back to that night … and the moment that neither of us saw coming. "It was never your fault. That fucker had it coming." He lets out a heavy breath before pressing his hand against the glass where mine rested.

"The wait will be over soon. Tomorrow, we will be together and lead our own life."

I offer a polite smile, licking my lips as I nod my answer. "I wish we didn't have a barrier now. I wish I could touch you now … I miss everything about you."

As he sighs, I feel it in my nerves, my body suddenly feeling hypersensitive. Even with the glass between us, I can feel the heat of his hand against mine. I feel my breath hitch as I see his eyes turning dark and intense.

"Are you trying to tease me, baby?"

I gulp as my thighs clench together under the desk. Sweat droplets run down my neck as I suddenly feel the atmosphere turning hot.

With a dark, hungry look, he leans closer as if what he has to say next is only meant for me, for my ears only. He doesn't want the officers listening to him. "Did you wear such a short dress to come and tease me, knowing well that I wouldn't be able to touch you? If you think you can get away with it, then you have another thing coming your way when I get out of here."

The warning makes my insides clench. "Maybe …" I barely whisper.

"What a wanton monster I created from just one night. The moment I get out of here, there will be no running from me."

I know he means each and every word he says. Every word uttered from his mouth holds a promise. A promise to get what he wants. A promise to give me what I have been waiting for for so damn long.

"When are you going to be released tomorrow?"

He leans back with a smug grin. "I'm not going to tell."

My eyes widen in shock. Wait. What? "But why? I want to be here to pick you up."

"I know, but I don't want you here."

My heart sinks at the thought of him not wanting me to be here. I've waited so long for him, and spending one more day without him still feels like a nightmare.

"I'll come for you. You will stay at your home waiting for me, and I will come for you. I'll be in your arms soon, but you're just going to have to wait."

Before I can mutter my protest, the guard comes and stands beside him. "Time's up. Let's go," he orders, but Parker doesn't move an inch as his eyes are trained on me only.

"I'll come for you, Angel," he whispers, kissing the bottom of the phone and winking at me. He places the phone back in its place and gets up, the guard following behind him. The entire time his gaze remains on mine. Not for a fleeting moment does his gaze falter until he leaves the room with the door closing behind him.

CHAPTER 4

I can feel the fresh burn of the tattoo on my skin, but I don't mind it at all. I never knew my night would go this way. I never expected this turn of events.

I still feel a bit tipsy from the drinks, but it doesn't stop me from smothering kisses on Parker's cheek as he unlocks the door to my hotel room so that I can get my stuff. Parker and I plan to stay the night at his hotel, and then I will spend the rest of my holiday with him. Luckily, I didn't run into my ex-boyfriend in the lobby.

I giggle as I stumble a little in the foyer even though Parker's arms are wrapped around me.

He snickers and kisses my temple before heading to the bedroom. "Where is your luggage?" he asks.

"Beside the nightstand."

He stalks toward the nightstand and retrieves my bag and other stuff from the bathroom. That's when the room door unlocks, and my ex-boyfriend enters.

"Logan?" I whisper.

"Where have you fucking been all day?" He sneers and marches over to me. His hands cup my shoulders with a tight grip while his nostrils flare with anger. "I've been going crazy here. Where have you been?"

Anger grips me as I push away his hands. "I was definitely cheating on you with your best friend."

His face pales as he gulps, nervousness pooling in his eyes.

"What? Got no excuses now?" I push against his chest.

He rolls his eyes and his jaw clenches. "It's not my fault you don't have enough time for me. I have needs too, but you are always so invested in your work that you forget about your damn boyfriend."

I shake my head in disbelief. "And that gives you the right to cheat?"

"Don't overreact so much. It was just one fucking night, so what?"

Before I know it, my hand lands on his right cheek with a harsh slap, making his head turn sideways. I don't know what possessed me to do so, but it gives me a sense of satisfaction. However, it only lasts for a fleeting moment, because he then charges at me and places his hands around my neck with a harsh grip. Right then, Parker emerges from the bedroom and takes in the scenario. Without wasting a minute, he pushes Logan away from me while I cough, begging for air.

"Stay the fuck away from her!" Parker growls, landing a punch on Logan's face and then his gut.

My ex falls to the ground with a grunt.

I take Parker's hand, stopping him from making the situation worse. "That's enough, Parker. Let's go."

Thankfully, he listens to me and grabs my bags as we head for the door. But what happens next is something I didn't expect. Logan instantly gets up and rushes Parker, landing two quick punches to his *face. Within seconds, they start fighting each other, but things get out of hand when I see the blood trickling down Parker's nose. Fear engulfs me as I look around for something, anything at all, to use to save Parker. My nerves start quivering with anxiety when I finally find something. I quickly pick up the vase from the corner table, and before I'm aware of what I'm doing, I smash it on Logan's head.*

His hands immediately go to his head as he grunts in pain and falls to the ground. I'm frozen in my spot as I watch the blood running like a river from his head as he lies still on the floor. I watch Parker kneel beside my ex and press two fingers against his pulse point. The minute I see his hand withdrawing and his head bowing down, guilt and fear crash over me.

He is dead … I killed him … What have I done? I can't breathe or think as I am lost in a daze. Suddenly, I feel Parker's hands shaking my shoulder, bringing me back to reality.

"I-I … I didn't mean to do it … he … h-he was attacking you, and I …" I stutter, unable to find the right words to speak my mind.

He cups my face, giving me an intense and serious look. "You didn't do anything. It's not your fault. You didn't kill him. I did."

⁂

The beeping of the alarm wakes me up. The memory is still so vivid. I could never forget that night. Unfortunately, during our moment, one of the hotel cleaners came into the room and immediately called the manager and the cops. And Parker? He took the blame for all of it and was sentenced to two years in prison.

Since that night, I have blamed myself for ruining his life, even though he told me not to. He told me to not let the past consume me and that I should move on, live my life. Most of all, he reminded me that I should never forget about him, because I owe him for saving my life and that he will be back to get what belongs to him—me.

CHAPTER 5

I keep twisting and turning in my bed. Sleep is not going to be my reprieve. I am far too restless to sleep. Today is the day that Parker is to be released, but I have not heard from him. He told me to wait, and I've been waiting for half of the day now. There is still no sign of him.

Throwing back the covers, I get up from the bed and stalk toward the kitchen. I grab a glass, fill it with water, and finish it instantly. My nerves calm for a few moments, but it doesn't last long. I let out a heavy sigh as I close my eyes. When will he be here? When?

A knock at the front door makes me jolt in surprise. It is a hard, heavy knock. I rush to the door knowing well who it could be. It has to be him. As I look through the peephole, I find the person I've been waiting for for two long years standing there.

The moment I unlock the door, I rush into his arms and wrap my arms around his neck. My pulsing heartbeat finally calms down as I relish the warmth of his body. He is finally here. Parker is back.

"I missed you so much. I missed this," he murmurs against my temple.

I nod as tears of joy streak down my cheeks. I have no words that can describe my happiness. "Please, never leave me again. I won't be able to survive …" My voice fades away.

"Never, Angel, and tonight, I'll make sure of it." He lifts me up in his arms, closing the door with a push of his feet, and takes me to my bedroom. He places me on the edge of the bed and kneels right in front of me.

I frown in confusion. "What is it, Parker? Where have you been all day?" I ask.

"I was freed in the morning, but I had to get something for my angel. Something to mark her as mine," he whispers and takes a box out from his pocket.

I gasp. My lips part and my eyes widen in utter surprise.

Presenting the box on his palm, he opens it and shows me the most beautiful emerald ring that I have ever seen. A square-shaped, green stone sits on the ring like it's a throne.

"With every passing day in prison, I missed you more and more. I thought of you every single second these past two years. You were stained in my memories every day, and bit by bit, I fell in love with you even more. Tonight, I want to have what's mine. I want to mark you. Be mine. Marry me, Angel."

My hands cup my mouth as fresh tears emerge from my eyes. I am overwhelmed with joy. "Yes. Yes! A million times yes," I mutter between sniffles.

He grins, takes out the ring, and puts it where it belongs. "Perfection. Just like you," he murmurs and presses his lips on mine, sealing the deal … making me his, marking me.

"Parker," I moan, my hands grabbing fistfuls of his hair, bringing him closer.

"You are all mine now, and I'm yours. We are both stained by each other. Forever."

Right away, he pushes me, my back hitting the soft bed cushion before he kneels between my thighs. He bends down and tears apart my panties and discards my T-shirt, making me gasp and whimper in seconds. He kisses and nips my thighs, then my stomach. He keeps stimulating my clit with his fingers as he crawls up my body, sucking the flesh along the way. His mouth closes over my nipple, and I lose it.

Arching my back and screwing my eyes shut, I moan out his name while he teases me. My eyes open to find Parker hovering over my body, his hair already a mess from my tight grip.

"I can't wait anymore. I need you right fucking now," he growls and unzips his pants. He takes out his raging erection and rubs it against my wet clit.

"Ah! Please, Parker," I beg.

Luckily, he takes pity on me, and with one thrust, he starts to fuck me. My legs immediately wrap around his waist as we both scream and moan each other's names, begging for more, wanting more.

This is our new beginning, as we promise to belong to each other forever. Our love marks us as our hearts are stained by the other.

Power Demands Passion

H.R. Hypolita

CHAPTER 1

"I don't need this shit! I quit!" Robyn Tanhill stormed out of her boss's office, her tall, strong frame quaking visibly. "I've taken enough garbage from this place to last a thousand years!" Mark had made one too many passes at her, and he finally made her an ultimatum. "And I wouldn't blow you with a vacuum cleaner, you fat little prick!"

Heads started popping up in various cubicles. The call center never needed an excuse for gossip, and Robyn knew it. Time to give them some new meat. "If you want to get blown so damn bad, just get another Thai escort!" She had been his secretary; she knew which calls to screen and which to allow through. "Only this time, don't be ashamed that your hooker had a cock!"

The call center stood silent. All the employees' heads were now up and out of their cubicles. Stupid Carl with his mustache, that nasty, gum-snapping Tanya, and the rest of the call center all looked at her with dull, lifeless eyes.

"You owe three hundred bucks to a lady-boy, and you're hassling me about some head? Fuck you!"

Smiles began growing out of gaping mouths, and then all at once, like a school of fish, they turned to look at Mark Stevens, assistant manager of Consolidated Collections call center. Mark attempted to fix his greasy hair and look in charge, his cheap tan suit a size too big. His spectacles drooped on his face from where Robyn had slapped him.

"Fuck you all!" she shouted as she grabbed her purse. "Mark, I hope that hooker gave you syphilis and that it kills you!" Robyn slammed the plate glass door, cracking it as she left the hellhole of a job for the last time.

She walked quickly through the parking lot. In the ruckus on her way out, she grabbed a company laptop. She considered it severance pay. Her yellow jacket fluttered in the breeze, and her red four-inch heels clicked and clacked as she made her way to her way to the Hornet, her little green Miata. She unbuttoned the jacket and tossed it in the passenger seat along with her purse and the Mac. She took off her heels, hopped in the driver's seat, and peeled out, leaving a long line of rubber in the parking lot.

Robyn loved the Hornet. Right after college, she'd bought the roadster used. The Hornet had been her graduation gift to herself. Her future looked rosy, and her designs would land her an amazing job. Certainly, a big firm in Manhattan or Chicago would hire her quickly. Seven years of compromise later, she'd just quit her ninth job, scraping by in Dayton, Ohio.

She hurled the little car down Webster Avenue. Dayton fucking Ohio was nothing but low-end office parks, gas stations, and pawnshops as far as the eye could see. The sickly-sweet odor of rendered corn from the Cargill plant filled her nose. Robyn drove on; she had to escape the stench of rendered corn. The fake sugar funk permeated every molecule of the area. Robyn downshifted and stepped on the gas. The little car roared with joy as she sped north. Driving faster and faster, she headed away from The Gem City with all haste.

Dayton had not been a gem in quite some time; a city of bones, no muscle, no meat, just bones were left. The gems were mined out a long time ago. Where industry once stood, rusted bones remained, barely grasping on to life. She had to keep driving. She didn't want to go home to her shitty apartment—not yet. Not ever, really. She had the Hornet, and she loved it, for it was the one thing in the world that could be called her own.

Small-minded individuals called it a dyke's car. She hated the term; besides, her Miata wasn't white, so the argument became moot. British racing green covered this little convertible as it tore up the road, out of the city, and into the flat Ohio suburban sprawl. She'd been with a few women, mostly in college, and she enjoyed it, but she liked a good hard cock more. She still hated the term *dyke*. The word held harsh and cutting letters. She didn't care who she fucked; she just fucked who she cared about, whether it was for a day or for a year.

She drove north, past the Air Force base and all those handsome pilots, past the University, and out into the farmland of Southwestern Ohio. She just kept on driving. The top down on the convertible blew her auburn hair back, and it felt great. The trees and farms with endless rows of corn and soybeans zipped by. She didn't want to go home yet. There was nothing to go home to anyway. No man, no woman, no cat. Nothing.

Robyn slowed the Hornet down, the realization of her predicament starting to settle in her mind. She didn't have anything. Quitting another job in a dramatic huff had become standard practice. Her student loan debt flashed to the front of her mind. She had every creditor's number memorized in her phone. There were at least eight. One number came from her very own call center! She pulled the car into a gas station, her thoughts reeling on her current situation. It couldn't be any direr; she had forty-seven thousand in student debt, five grand more in credit cards, rent, food, and no job. She needed a drink and to clear her head.

Robyn took a deep breath and exited the car. Her heels, back on her feet, flashed red and shiny in the June sunshine, crunching the gravel with each determined step. Around her, the green of soybeans and corn stretched out for miles, and in front of her stood a rundown, two-pump gas station. The door jingled as she entered the convenient store. She walked straight to the back, grabbed a bottle of screw-top Shiraz, and walked to the counter.

The young clerk had his eyes glued on her since the moment she pulled up outside. Clearly, they don't get women who look like her out here in the sticks. She liked how he looked at her, horny, yet harmless. He was just some dumb kid, eighteen tops. He still had pimples. She towered over him at five foot ten. He could only look at her, his eyes glued to every bend and arc of her statuesque body. Her full breasts pressed proudly against her silk blouse. The deep curves of her waist, hips, and round ass all made for the full female package.

"Pack of Philly Blunts too," Robyn said.

"D-do you need matches?" the kid asked, wearing his ballcap flat-billed, like a hayseed. Hayseed's nametag read Jimmy.

"No. I'll take a lighter, though, Jimmy."

"Yy-yes ma'am."

Now she felt old. He grabbed a white mini Bic.

"That big black one will fit my hand just fine." She smiled. "Jimmy."

"That will be nine thirty-five."

Robyn dropped a ten on the counter, grabbed her wine and smokes, turned on her heel, and strutted to the door. She can start counting change tomorrow. Restarting life will begin tomorrow. Hell, it worked for Scarlett O'Hara. She walked out the door with a jiggle and could feel Jimmy's eyes on her bottom as she walked out. She enjoyed having men look at her ass; it gave her a sense of power and control.

The Hornet started up again, and she peeled out of the parking lot and continued north, now with a smile on her face for the first time that day. It felt like the first time in weeks. She felt sexy again, if just for a moment, and it felt nice. She loved to play head games. They were fun and mostly harmless, but not always. Games gave Robyn a feeling of power and dominance.

She tried it in the sack with a few guys, dominating them, but had no real takers. Some would talk a big game. Men will say anything if they think it will get you to fuck them. So, she just turned it on them. Robyn could flip a man in three moves; she held a black belt in Aikido. Sex, fucking, all of it became a chess game, move and countermove.

This might not be the healthiest view of couplehood and love, but it certainly worked in the world of Tinder and online dating. Move and countermove, keep the other one guessing. Get close enough to hurt, but keep enough distance to protect yourself. Move and countermove.

Robyn smiled and remembered Dave, the car dealer. Dave panicked. His profile said he was up for "whatever." So much for being open-minded. Apparently, you have to get written consent to tie up a grown man and fuck him in this day and age. "Pussy," she muttered to herself.

She had tied both his arms to the bed when he started to sweat. His left leg started visibly shaking when she reached for it. He had a conniption fit when she placed a wet thumb *on*, not even *in* his ass. The idiot tried to wrench his arm free; instead, he dislocated it and passed out.

His wife picked him up from the hospital. Robyn didn't know he had a wife. Robyn didn't really care either. She dropped him off and drove away. She found him on Tinder and swiped right. It's not her fault he forgot the safe word, or that he lied. Or did *she* forget? It didn't really matter anyway; he lied, and the universe punished him. Karma is a bitch.

She drove on, heading toward Glen Helen Preserve, only a few miles away. It was one of the few old-growth forests left in Southwestern Ohio. How the hell had she ended up here in Dayton? She had a degree from DePaul, and she had an excellent design portfolio, yet she just quit a miserable secretary job for the ninth time. Could it be fear?

She didn't even freelance anymore. The stupid fucking job sucked all her energy out. These jobs were the backup plan. Her future plans were to do cover art for games and books, not getting coffee and screening for hookers in a call center. Robyn hadn't picked up a brush or a pencil in months. She moved from Chicago to Indianapolis to Dayton. Fuck! Why? Low rent? Some guy? Some girl? Why?

"Seven years of fucking compromise! Now I'm looking at the short end of thirty, with nothing to show for it!" She pulled into Glen Helen. Its ancient trees towered above her. Big, leafy oaks and poplars had stood here for hundreds of years. The preserve always held a wonderful stillness. She needed to get a little air, have a drink, and walk. Robyn just needed to walk. There were no cars around.

Robyn opened her purse, pulled out her glass one-hitter loaded with Trainwreck, and lit up. The pot calmed her jangled nerves. She had more at home and would roll up a blunt then. The one-hitter would have to do for now. She took a few more puffs of the pipe and dropped it in her jacket pocket. Robyn then took off her heels and put on her Nikes. She grabbed the bottle of wine, donned the jacket, and stepped out of the Hornet.

The gravel of the empty parking lot crunched under her feet. There were no cars, bikes, or joggers. There was nothing but the sound of the wind blowing through the trees and the smell of wildflowers. Behind her lay farmland as far she could see, but before her rose the forest, ancient and dark. The great oaks rose from the plains before her like old gods. They creaked and groaned with each gentle breeze. The shadows of the forest cooled her warm skin almost immediately. The cap of the wine popped and clicked as she opened it with one twist.

"I'm one classy lady," she muttered to herself, then took a drink straight from the bottle. She took another pull of wine and continued her walk. The forest had been here for a very long time. Massive oaks, poplars, and elms were everywhere. The density of the trees limited her visibility, and she could only see a few feet past the trail. The early summer had been kind to the preserve. Wildflowers added explosions of color; purples and golds, whites, and blues dotted the green expanse.

Robyn knew she was alone when she walked onto the forest trail. The trail wound up and down through Glen Helen, and the weed and wine wound up and down through her bloodstream. She could feel the beginning of a nice buzz. Robyn had been to Glen Helen a dozen times; still, the place felt new to her each visit.

She walked along the trail, following the path's rises and descents. The trail's twists and turns brought new beauties around each corner—wildflowers in bloom, rabbits feeding on clover, and bluebirds singing for a spring mate. Robyn, feeling the full effect of Shiraz and a good high, began to finally relax. The morning's events began to slip away, another shitty job lost in a long stretch of shitty jobs. She would do one of two things—find a new shitty job, or not.

Could she embrace the fear of not working some garbage job? Robyn knew there were far worse rock bottoms than walking out of a call center after being propositioned by an asshole for sex. She had her designs, her portfolio, and her drawings, so why not? This could be a starting point for a whole new career, one she'd dreamed of for a long time. This could be her empire-building moment!

Her confidence immediately began to swell up after months of bruising. Robyn's long legs moved a little faster as she continued through the forest, moving from a walk to a stride. A smile slid across her face. Her new life started right now. The breeze blew across her smooth skin, and it felt like a blessing.

The trail arrived at a small creek, a *crick* in the South, no wider than a girl could jump. The moving water glinted in the dappled sun like diamonds. The water popped and gurgled in a pleasing pattern, moving and tumbling over rocks and branches, heading to the Miami River, the Ohio, Mississippi, and, eventually, the Atlantic. There had been no rain for the last week, and the ground stood dry, so Robyn risked her Nikes, her balance, and her Shiraz as she went off the trail and followed the creek.

The creek gurgled and giggled at her as she traipsed across the forest floor and up the stream's banks. Feelings of pride and confidence began to surge within her. Quitting her job could be the best thing that could happen! "Everything feels new," she said quietly. "I'll sue the fuck out of him." At nine a.m. tomorrow, she'll start looking for lawyers. Today, she'll drink, walk in the woods, and think of the future.

The creek slowly led up a hillock. A small waterfall poured over the side. She dipped her hands into the warm, rushing water. Warm? There must be a spring nearby! She scrambled up the hill and saw a stunning azure pond. The pool, breathtaking in its beauty, had an inviting quality. It was tucked into the side of the hill. She'd never seen such a deep blue before, maybe on Lake Superior, but certainly not in a tiny little pond. The burble of the water and the warmth from the spring sent a wave of relaxation over her. Robyn took off her Nikes and dipped her toe into the warm water. It was quite warm, actually, with a pleasurable tingle. It was almost hot, like a relaxing spa. She'd heard of the therapeutic nature of warm springs, and she loved a good mud bath.

"Why not?" she said aloud. The pool could not be seen from any trail, as it was surrounded by boulders and dense trees. Why not take a dip? It was as if the spring was calling to her, tempting her. Robyn gingerly looked into the pool and immediately felt her body being drawn in. She liked the feeling in the pit of her stomach as it pulled on her.

She dipped her big toe into the water again. The pleasing tingle in her toe increased immediately. She pulled it back out in shock. The water still called to her, and her body began calling back. The energy in her stomach had begun to spread into her chest, hips, and her warming pussy. The toe felt as if it had been massaged by tiny experts. She placed the tingling digit back into the warm, limpid pool, and let out a shocked moan. The water felt so good that it gave her a jolt of pure pleasure. She could feel her arousal building in her very core. Robyn wanted more.

"I'll just have a quick dip." Her big toe felt fully awake, and she focused on the wonderful feelings the water was giving her. Robyn's foot entered the pool, and the pleasing tingles spread and increased in intensity. As the water began to cover more of her foot, the better it felt, and the more intense the need to be fully in the pool. She could hear a high-pitched and pleasurable hum as her left foot went into the spring. Robyn's pleasure instantly doubled. Another sharp moan escaped her surprised lips.

"What is happening to me?" she whispered, her hands beginning to caress the curves of her breasts. The yearning for more pleasure was becoming uncontrollable. She could feel her hands unbuttoning her jacket, yet she had no control over its removal. The bright-yellow coat fell to the ground in a canary-colored heap.

The message her feet were sending to her brain couldn't be clearer. *Remove your clothes. Get in the spring. Swim in the pond.* Her long, strong calves, when hit with the water, started sending lightning bolts of information into her pussy, her clit, and her brain. *Remove your clothes. Get in the spring. Swim in the pond.*

There was not a soul for miles. She took a big swig of wine. Robyn's feet and her red-painted toenails tingled with excitement as her strong calves twitched in sexual anticipation. She began to remove her silk blouse, her long fingers fumbling with the mother of pearl buttons. "Fuck it!" she tore the blouse off, sending a shower of buttons into the pool. The warm air felt good on her bare, toned midriff. She tossed the remains of the blouse onto a nearby lilac bush.

The perfume from the flowers only contributed to her newfound passion. She felt a wave of excitement crash over her. Robyn knew she was becoming swept away by this new passion, this new desire. She couldn't get her clothes off fast enough. Her pencil skirt came off so fast the zipper tore, and she threw the offending skirt into the woods. "Fuck it! I never want to own office wear again!"

A woman possessed, she had to get in that water. The filthy urges coursing through her body took control. It felt all-possessing, consuming her, calling to her body, and her body responded in kind. Her silk panties were starting to dampen as her breasts swelled and strained against her silk brassiere. She stood before the beautiful spring, her dark lingerie clashing with her creamy skin, distorted by the ripples of the water.

She was a woman possessed by a powerful unknown force. The ripples of the pond danced and lapped at the edge. Her body looked different in the reflection, better than usual, taller, and stronger. Robyn took care of herself, ran 5ks, and biked, but this reflection appeared more as an ideal mirror. She blinked and looked at her reflection in the pond again. She looked amazing to behold. Tall and powerful, she was a goddess of old, like Diana or Kali. "I should be holding a fucking spear," she said as she admired herself.

Robyn unhooked the front clasp of the black bra and felt the weight of her large breasts as the cool air hit her dark nipples. Her mind blurred between the knowledge that her body was experiencing the impossible, and the unstoppable need to be in the water, to feel its warmth caressing and surrounding her needing body. Her nipples hardened so quickly it made her gasp. She had to swim in this spring. Right here and now, she must have more of the water covering her body. The wind caught her dark hair as she took off her panties, exposing her trimmed pussy to the June air. She stood before the pond, naked and powerful, a woman in full.

Get in the pond. Swim in the water.

Robyn looked into the pond and dove in headfirst. The final moment before the water enveloped her felt like an eternity without a lover's kiss. The warm June morning rushing over her toned and naked body as she sprung up into the air. Anticipation shot through her as her heart pounded away in her heaving chest. She entered the water as if she was a creature of the sea. The gurgling sounds disappeared as her hands and arms broke the surface. When they did, the energy and passion in her body began to build deep within her bones and soul.

The heat of the water surrounded her like a lover. The spring enveloped her, warm and embracing. She immediately became awake, alive, and powerful. Her head broke the surface, and it spun wildly with activity. Robyn became aware of her entire body all at once; she understood her heartbeat and could see her breathing. Her mind raced across an open plain from which she could see forever, and it all focused on pleasure.

The lightning bolts that shot through her calves were now coming from all her limbs. The bolts coursed through her and ended with a rhythmic thud, deep in her yearning, hot pussy. As these bolts drummed through her body, she could see in her mind's eye an orgasm of beautiful proportions, just beyond the corners of her vision. Her areolas snapped to attention. They were so hard, they were almost vibrating. She thought she'd come right then and there, only to realize that this feeling only hinted at the pleasure she would feel.

She wanted more. Her body tingled from her toes to her tits to the top of her head. The vibrations were in all places at once. Even the water of the warm spring seemed to vibrate. She dove in again and looked around the pond. The water, clear as a diamond, looked to her as if she was wearing goggles. Robyn could see all the details of the spring floor. The pool extended down deeper than she expected, and it was far more lovely. Robyn's body demanded that she touch the bottom.

Her head broke the surface once again, and her body felt the pleasure and need increase to a fevered pitch. No weed or wine caused this wonderful euphoria. Something new, something powerful drew on her yearning, horny mind and body. She could feel the desire in her head, in her neck, and in her very erect nipples.

The messages coming from pussy were very clear. *Rub me, pinch me, fuck me until I come, and do it now.*

She felt like a horny teenager again with her pussy screaming to be touched, clit throbbing, and lips wet from deep, filthy need and the power of the pool. Her mind and body pleaded for her fingers to find new ways to her most sensitive of places. Her fingers found their way home very quickly. The first graze of her clit sent shock waves through her. She gasped and stopped. Robyn, not being a stranger to fingerfucking herself, had never felt such a surge of pleasure and need. She started again in earnest, rubbing harder and faster.

Swim in the water. Swim to the bottom.

Robyn took a deep breath and dove. She had one hand on her pussy, her fingers working like crazy, and her other hand squeezing her tits together. It all felt so good. *Can I come before I run out of air?* The thought shot through her head like an arrow.

Everything felt right as she kicked down to the bottom of the pond. She could feel her lungs immediately begin to call for air, but she didn't care. She needed to come more than breathe. She needed to come hard. Her fingers slid in and out of her pussy, three at a time. She could fit four. She pushed the folds of her sex open and slipped in her four left fingers, her thumb rubbing her clit. Four fingers moved at a breakneck pace in and out of her swollen and slippery mound. Harder and faster, she worked her tight, hot pussy.

Her lungs were screaming for air. She didn't care about living or breathing, she just needed to come. Robyn let go of her breasts and latched onto the bottom of the pond with her right hand. The water was so clear, so warm. It filled her with sexual energy. The spring filled Robyn with new strength and a raw, untamed power. She could feel her orgasm brewing. She never had a problem coming when she wanted it, and she wanted to come right now.

Tiny bubbles of air floated up as she held her breath while grunting and fucking herself like a wild animal. The race to the finish line between her pussy and her lungs continued. Robyn's lungs were screaming, but the rest of her body started screaming louder. Fingers worked their magic with the enchantment of the water, sliding over every fold of her sex. Her ring, pinky, and middle fingers were shoved deep inside her, while index and thumb worked her bellowing, horny, hot clit.

Her head spun in wild loops. Her pussy was an inferno in the hot water of the spring. Robyn's lungs were screaming as she came. A light burned so brightly behind her eyelids that she could see the capillaries behind her eyes. She could see her power, her pleasure, her orgasm, and time itself stood still for a single, perfect moment in the dark, warm silence below the surface of the spring.

Robyn came in a new way, her body electrified by the surging, throbbing pleasure of the spring. Thunderbolts shot through her body. Her fingers flew, pushing more pleasure from her pussy into her womanly core. The pleasure surged and rolled like bubbling lava rolling through her system. She kept coming. It wouldn't stop. She couldn't stop. Her orgasm rolled over her, up from her toes to her knees, through her pussy and ass, across her tight stomach, up her tits, and through her rock- hard nipples.

Each nipple began vibrating on its own frequency, each areola giving a different joy to her body and mind. Her stomach filled with butterflies. Hopscotched lines of undulating, wet, pink, orgasmic waves moved up from her throbbing cunt through her spine, back, heaving breasts, and into her filthy, waiting mind. Robyn's id sent those waves right back down through her titties and into her pussy, clitoris, and ass. It was a closed loop of wet, filthy, orgasmic hedonism, all contained in her body. She became lightning in a bottle, the thunderbolts desperate to break free and run forever across a golden plain of filthy, needy pleasure.

The orgasm tore through her brain like a wrecking ball. She could feel it in her skull as she screamed out. Her grip slipped from the rock, and she shot to the surface. Screaming, still coming, she felt the waves of joy, pain, and unquenchable pleasure coursing through her. She would have stayed under the water forever if she could. She'd done a little choking before, but nothing like this. This was like being fucked by the universe itself. Red borders began building behind her closed eyes. The waves of filth, fuck, and joy began to subside, and she couldn't take any more from herself.

Robyn burst through the surface of the pool with a shriek of victory, her body triumphant, a pillar of sexual power. She could feel that power coursing through her veins. She made her way to the end of the pond, quivering with newfound energy. Her senses were heightened. She felt stronger. She could hear farther, smell the tiniest flower in a hayfield miles away, see deeper into the forest, and could even hear dragonflies buzz and hum.

She noticed three things right away. One, her clothes were missing. Two, only ten feet from her stood the biggest horse she'd ever seen. Three, an angular and armored blond man stood staring at her with a look of total shock across his handsome face.

Chapter 2

The blond man stood tall, towering, and lean. His long hair fell around him like a cape, with a single thick braid over the top of his head. His angled face with a chin to cut glass held an expression of shock. No one could be more surprised than him when a tall, nude human popped out of the pond he happened to be watering his horse at.

"Who the fuck are you?" Robyn exclaimed. "What the fuck did you do with my clothes?" She stormed out of the water, not bothering to cover herself. She had just had the greatest orgasm in existence, and this stranger would not be ruining that today.

"Back, naiad!" The strange man stumbled backward. "I mean you no harm!" He tripped over a gnarled tree root and fell, landing with a thump.

He tried to scramble away, but Robyn pounced on him in a flash. She pinned his arms to the unyielding turf. He'd never seen a woman move so quickly or have such strength.

"Where are my fucking clothes?"

He tried to push away, but she held him firmly. Robyn could feel the power coursing through her arms. She could break his arm in a pinch.

"Please, I know not of your clothes. I did not steal them … My name is Kivik. I just stopped to water Tullsta, my horse."

Robyn looked deep into Kivik's blue eyes. He told the truth. She let go of his arms but didn't get off him. Not yet. "Did you see any kids or college students fucking around with my stuff?"

"College students? I am unaware of that tribe. Are they hill folk or cave dwellers?" Kivik replied quizzically.

"You didn't see anyone?" Robyn asked.

"Nay. I'm traveling to Variara to offer my services. There are few travelers on this road; Stocksund Forest can be quite dangerous."

This answer caught Robyn off-guard. "Variara? Stocksund Forest? Are you a goddamn role player? Break fucking character, asshole. My clothes, my purse, cell phone, car keys … fuck! I'm fucked!"

Robyn stood and began looking around the pond. Nothing remained; she must have been robbed. Only at this moment did she realize the precariousness of her situation. It was just her and the strange man called Kivik. She gave him a good long look. His costume was better than anything she'd seen at the Renaissance Festival. He wore a leather doublet of the finest quality, clearly hand-tooled with weaving vines details. His breeches were also made out of leather, this time woven into delicate cords with intricate details of leaves and birds. Filigree of silver and gold curled down through the seams, splits, and gaps. His legs looked as if they were covered in vines made of precious metal. He looked like one of her portfolio mockups. Hell, he had his own massive horse.

The destrier stood above the two of them. Her thick neck bulged with strength. The sun caught the dark-brown coat and made the great mare sparkle in the daylight. A narrow white blaze decorated her forehead and snout. She stood a full eighteen hands high, making her the biggest horse Robyn had ever seen. A thick, wispy tail snapped to and fro, calming Robyn slightly.

"You wouldn't happen to have a spare costume, would you? At least a blanket? What you say your name was? Kivik?"

"I do." His doublet heaved with his breathing.

The light of the sun caught all matter of stamped and carved imagery across his chest. The strange man bore tales of conquest, battle, and triumph on his clothes. He wore a long dagger as well. Robyn wished she'd seen that before she tackled him. The scabbard bore the same wire filigree as his breeches, weaving vines of silver through dark, hardened leather. Kivik vaulted to his feet with surprising agility, considering he had been tackled by a beautiful, naked, unarmed woman. He went to his horse and pulled a heavy cloak from the saddle.

The forest stood silent. No birds were chirping anymore. Robyn looked around. All was silent. The waterfall!

"What happened to the waterfall?" She looked at the pond. This water stood still as glass. The rocks were jagged and bare, not rounded and mossy. "Where is the waterfall? The hill? The fucking creek? Where am I?" Robyn asked as she grabbed the cloak and wrapped herself quickly, the warm, soft fabric comfortable against her skin.

Kivik looked at her. "On the road to Variara in Stocksund Forest. Are you not a naiad of this pool?"

"Please drop the act, Jamie Lannister. Where am I?" Where the fuck am I?"

"As I stated, the road between Variara and Forvara in Stocksund Forest."

"Stop saying that. Where am I?"

"My lady, I only speak the truth. We elves are sworn to truth and beauty above all else."

Robyn took a step back. "Elves?"

Kivik pulled back his great mane of blond hair to reveal a sharply-pointed ear. "Kivik of Muren, at your service. I take it from your expression that you have never met any of the high folk before. You must be from a very small village; we're quite common. Is it nearby? It would be my honor to help you find your way home."

"I have a feeling my home is very, very far away." Robyn's head began to reel. An elf! She just spoke to an elf.

Robyn looked at Kivik again; he had beautiful, strong features, with a chin you could cut a diamond upon, and yet was feminine and graceful. She could still feel the power of the pool coursing through her veins, the passion and filthy lust that took over her mind and body, the desperate and rising tingle, and the flash of light when she came. The pool brought her here. Maybe it could bring her back! The pool could take her home!

Robyn threw the cloak to Kivik. Naked once again, she dove into the pool. The water hit her body in a warm flash. Her head broke the surface without a single ripple. Robyn took in a huge gulp of air and dove. Her ass and legs shot up and disappeared below the surface.

Kivik stood there, gaping. He'd never seen a woman with such speed and strength before, certainly not a human woman. Kivik, a First Spear of the Line, who had fought in countless battles with bandits, ogres, humans, halflings, and minotaurs, had never been bested. He'd fought at the clash of the Bend when all thought lost, his spearmen almost overwhelmed by a horde of spider mounts, only to rally forth and claim victory. He had slain foes by the score, had fallen to his spear and dagger in single combat, and never once been bested—except for moments ago when this goddess tackled him.

The water goddess defeated him in moments. Not in sixty years of combat had he been bested, yet a naked human woman, one stunningly powerful, nude, human woman, defeated him. When she held his wrists, she could have broken them. He could feel her strength and her power. He should have been scared; instead, Kivik felt excitement as he watched her run into the pool and disappear. She just threw his cloak to him and took off as if he was a servant. It was all very confusing, yet all very exciting.

The water did not move. Kivik looked on. Had she hit her head? Perhaps she trapped her foot? Quickly, he began untying his doublet. He threw the leather protection away and pulled off his shirt in a flash to reveal his strong, muscular frame. His body was marked with scars from countless battles and fallen enemies. He stripped off his boots and ran toward the water.

He dove in, barely making a splash, and kicked down into the pool toward the beautiful woman at the bottom. He could just barely make out her stunning form in the darkness. He reached out for her. She had her left hand buried between her legs, and her right hand latched onto a rock. Kivik grabbed her under the arm and pushed up off the bottom.

Robyn held tight to the pond floor. She had to get home. Her fingers were flying over her hot clit and pussy. She had to come, and she had to get home. No one was going to stop her. Her lungs were screaming. Her pussy ached for a second release. Kivik's hand moved under her arm. They locked eyes under the water. Her left hand still furiously worked her pussy into a wet mess. Another orgasm brewed up deep inside her, bigger than before. Her right hand held onto the rock for dear life.

Kivik couldn't unlatch the woman. By the gods, she had strength. He'd never encountered such power in a creature before, certainly none so strange and passionate as this goddess. His lungs started asking for air as he grabbed her with both hands and kicked off the bottom of the pond.

Robyn's pussy screamed for release, her clit engorged and raging. She had four fingers jammed up her slick, wet pussy, while this blond god of a man tried to pull her up out of the pool. What was he doing? Robyn released her right hand, wrapped it around Kivik's neck, and kissed him deeply. Her tongue and his swirled together, lighting tiny sparks of passion in both their mouths.

The orgasm hit the next moment. It broke free of her pussy like a raging bomb. It shook through her entire skeleton, rattling her bones and clacking her teeth. They shot to the surface in great haste.

"Agh! Fuck!" Robyn screams were unearthly. The two lovers broke the surface of the water, the rolling, wet orgasm thundering through her very bones. "What the fuck do you think you are doing?"

"Saving you from drowning?"

Those were the last words spoken. Robyn moved on Kivik like a wraith. She kissed him hard on the mouth.

Pausing for a moment, she said, "I need you to fuck me, Kivik. I need you to fuck me now—and I better come." Robyn felt the sexual power coursing through her veins. She would take this elf. "I'll worry about the consequences tomorrow. Right now, I need you to fuck me. Right here and right now." Besides, she thought, Scarlet O'Hara would fuck a hot elf too.

She slid her wet hand down his bare chest and wrapped her long, strong legs around him. "I need you to please me, Kivik." She kissed him again, her tongue meeting his. She could feel the sparks again as their tongues danced together.

Her eyes were blue fire. Kivik's cock suddenly started to grow with every word the strange goddess said. She reached into his trousers, grabbed ahold, and began to stroke his hard shaft. Elven cocks, she thought, are quite large, with a good solid girth, and growing larger by the second.

"I think this will do just fine." She stared into his eyes. He looked back enraptured by her, powerless to do anything but obey. She stroked his cock faster. "Are you going to fuck me, Kivik? Are you going to please me?"

"Yes" was the only word Kivik could grunt.

Her hand felt strong, yet supple as she stroked his long, thick shaft with determined action. It moved with an expert grace that not even high court mistresses and courtesans could boast about. He shed his trousers while still in the water and put two long, thick fingers against the waiting entrance to her tight, warm pussy.

"*Oh*, fuck, yes. Good boy, Kivik. Work my pussyhole."

His hands were strong, and Robyn wrapped her legs around his taut frame. She started working her hips against his hand. Harder and faster, she bounced on his long, strong fingers. Her arms were wrapped around Kivik's broad shoulders. They were looking into each other's eyes.

"Suck my titties, boy. Suck 'em hard." She rose up on his chest and placed one nipple up to his mouth.

Kivik placed his lips on her perfect nipple. He brushed it at first. It was ruby hard and just as red. He bit down, and Robyn moaned in pleasure. Kivik had never seen such breasts. They were full, round peaks capped with dark, sensitive nipples. Where did this goddess come from? The elf could feel his mind becoming ensnared in her web. He was falling under her spell.

While Kivik licked and sucked Robyn's nipple, her hand continued working his cock with fervor. It was not quite like a human cock, she thought, but somehow both stronger and more delicate. It was a cock made by an artist rather than a craftsman, and it felt good in her hand. Robyn desperately wanted it in her pussy and ass.

Kivik had both nipples in his mouth now, holding Robyn's big, firm tits in one hand while fingerfucking her with the other. Her hips and pussy were banging off his hand while she maintained a rock-hard grip on his hard cock. Worked by her hand, the elven member was now a hardened agate of sexual arousal. The human hand was more forceful than a delicate elven stroke. It moved up and down, squeezing his cock head and taking the whole shaft in a stroke. He could feel his orgasm rising from deep in his bowels. His cock grew and swelled again.

"Not yet, boy. I'm not done with you yet." Robyn let go of Kivik's pulsing member. "Now, you take a deep breath and eat my pussy." She put her weight on his shoulders, forcing him down. She was a woman possessed with sexual power. The last thing Kivik heard before going under was simply, "Deep breath."

He found her warm, furious pussy and buried his face in it. The fuzzy lips tasted salty and sweet. Kivik felt her legs on his shoulders. She held him down to lick her womanly mound to orgasm. He had to make this goddess come. His life depended on it. He lapped away at her tender womanhood, a hungry wolf in full rut. With each lick on her hood and clit he could feel her shake more and more.

Robyn pushed her pussy into his mouth as she held Kivik's head down. "That's it, boy. You eat my pussy. Make me come." She'd never felt sex like this before. The forest was spinning, and the pond was as still as glass. "Lick my dirty pussy clean and make me—"

She didn't finish. Her third orgasm of the day lit her up like a pinball machine. It arrived without warning, but it was certainly a welcome addition to her collection. "*Oh*, fuck! Yes! Fuck!" Her screams echoed through the forest. Her legs opened up, and her arms released Kivik from her hot hole. "Fuck, boy! You sure can eat a pussy! Let's see if you can fuck as well as you eat."

Robyn straddled his waist as they floated together in the still pool. Kivik's turgid shaft waited, standing at attention like a good strong cock should. She pulled her legs apart as his long cock slid into her awaiting pussy.

"Oh, my god, my god, my god!" she exclaimed as Kivik began thrusting.

His strokes were long and strong. They ended with almost a thud at the base of her cunny tunnel. Robyn could feel the walls of her slit being stretched open. His cock just kept growing bigger and bigger. It filled her entire pussy. Kivik kissed her deeply as he bore down on her with his elvenhood. His blond mane swirled and tossed about, while her deep-brown hair was tossed back and slick to her skin. The water stood as still as glass.

Kivik fucked her as if on a mission. Robyn could feel his orgasm building, and his cock still growing. She could feel the walls of her cunny being stretched to an infinite point as the throbbing, thrusting cock of this warrior pressed home. She knew he would be coming soon, and that orgasm would be on her terms.

With each thrust, the elf grew more focused. His agate-hard prick yearned to burst forth and fill this goddess with his seed. Her fiery-hot pussy gripped his shaft with a vengeance. Her hips slammed into his as their sexes clashed. It was a timeless battle between willing combatants, one that never ends and is always won. His cock and her pussy were entwined. Thrust and parry, dodge and thrust. He could feel his orgasm begin to surge up out of his bowels and through his shaft.

Robyn could feel it too. She reached under his thick cock and past his heavy, silken balls. She placed two fingers near his ass. "I told you. You'll come on my terms, boy." With that, she pushed in on his ass.

Kivik looked at her with fear.

"Trust me. You're safe with me." Her fingers went deeper. She pushed past the resistance of his yielding ass. She took that resistance away. Her fingers started fucking his ass while her pussy fucked his cock. Her fingers pulsed away, seeking and hunting, determined to find their prize.

Kivik's mind spun from the sudden shift in power and pleasure. Her fingers in his ass sought his inner almond. Her pussy pulled his essence out. He arched his back as he felt a third finger push in. He wanted more. "Harder," he moaned.

"Harder what, boy?"

"Harder, please, my goddess."

Robyn had him. She pulled her hand out and made a duckbill with it. She looked into his blue eyes with her flaming gaze. "It starts like a duck, and it ends like a duck, but in the middle …" She shoved her hand into his tight, willing asshole. "It can be a fist." She pushed into his asshole hard.

Kivik's moan came from deep within him as his asshole pushed open and stretched. Robyn's fingers were long, her knuckles were wide, and Kivik's ass was tight and willing. In this singular moment, Kivik saw the thin line between pain and pleasure. He gasped as her hand just kept moving forward without pause. With each micron of movement, the elf became more aroused, more desperate. He could feel the base of her thumb inside of him. Her entire hand clenched in his ass, and he loved it.

Wrist deep in his tight asshole, Robyn found what she had been seeking. She ran her fingers over his prostate while fucking Kivik's ass with her fist. It was her ass now. She took it. She owned it. The goddess was in control, and he knew it. She could bend this beautiful man to her will and use his cock to tear up her pussy as she saw fit.

Kivik's heart skipped a beat as his asshole opened up. Her big fist was inside him, and his ass was stretched wide and willing. His eyes filled with starbursts as she clawed for his inner almond. She thrust into his ass while he pumped into her pussy. They were fucking each other on an almost equal plane. She towered above him, her dark hair slick to her glowing skin. She became, in this pure moment, his goddess. He would worship, defend, and follow her.

The forest stood silent, aside from the sound of two creatures in a deep rut. The primal and ancient sounds of hard, raw fucking echoed through the wooded landscape as the two beasts brought themselves to a shattering climax.

Robyn could feel Kivik's cock swell for the final push. She gritted her teeth as he bore into her, and Kivik clenched his jaw as she bore into him. The fucking defied physics; it didn't make sense in space or time, but both knew it to be perfect. He thrust into her cunny while she fucked his dick with her vibrant cunt. Robyn worked his ass and prostate like a puppet as his long, hard cock tore her pussy up and down. As his orgasm built to ever greater heights, Robyn's did as well.

"By the gods!" Kivik could feel himself beginning to come. He had never felt such a full-bodied orgasm before; he came from his cock, his ass, his balls, and his mind. He could feel it everywhere and all at once, a surging wave of pure pleasure rocking his brain and body. Kivik's load blasted up from deep in his cock and simply continued. His orgasm rolled over him as his cum leapt from his cockhead deep into Robyn's wet, hot waiting hole. His ass and prostate kept getting fucked harder, and he loved it. The feeling of a second, deeper orgasm building up in his asshole shocked him.

Robyn's fist fucked his ass harder while she rode his hard, spent cock. She wanted more from this elf. Robyn simply screamed, a deep, guttural announcement of nonsense as her pussy erupted in raw pleasure for the fourth time in an hour. She kept fucking his ass with her fist, and she kept fucking his cock with her pussy. The orgasm racked her body with spasms. She saw her own blood vessels behind her eyes again. When her pussy, finally satisfied, stopped quivering, she pulled her fist out of Kivik's gaping asshole, and slid off his limp and spent elven cock.

They held each other in silence, gasping for breath. The water of the pond was as still as glass and as warm as summer. Holding each other, they floated for what seemed like an eternity, too stunned to speak.

Eventually, Robyn blinked her eyes. She looked around the pond. Her clothes were still gone, and she remained stranded in this strange forest.

Kivik looked at her. His blue eyes were deep sapphires, while her eyes burned with a dark flame. "You are my goddess, and I will worship, defend, and honor you."

"Good. Because I have no fucking clue where I am, I have no clothes, no money, and no car."

They walked out of the pond, leaving nary a ripple. Naked, Kivik strode to his horse. Robyn admired his strong frame and wondered about the scars she saw. Who was this elf? Did she just fuck an elf? Did she just fist an elf? How does he know English? She planned on getting to the bottom of most of these questions; the rest, she accepted as fact.

Kivik dug out a pair of breeches and a shirt from his saddle pack. He handed them to Robyn. "Will these make do until we can acquire something more suitable, goddess?"

"These will do just fine. My name is Robyn. Robyn Tanhill. You don't have to call me goddess—unless I tell you to." She looked around at the forest, the pond, and Kivik. "Well, Kivik, you fuck amazing, and I love that trick your cock does."

Kivik took a little bow and smiled. He pulled up his trousers and tucked his magic dick away.

"I need to know a few things because I am a stranger here, and I think I'm going to be here for quite some time." Robyn said this right before she muttered to herself, "That doesn't sound so bad." Little did she know of the adventure that awaited her in the days and months ahead.

Chapter 3

"So, you're a soldier?" Robyn looked up from Kivik's supplies. Before her lay two swords, a bow of horn, a long silver spear, several daggers and knives, and a quiver full of white arrows.

"I am the First Spear of the Line," Kivik said with pride. He stood up tall as he said it, adding another inch to his already lengthy frame.

"That's good? Sounds good."

"Only the finest fighters in Muren are invited to the order of the First Spear. It's an ancient and sacred order, a great privilege."

Kivik's clothes didn't fit Robyn, resulting in constant tucking and adjusting. With no bra to wear, her breasts were loose under the shirt, and she caught Kivik stealing glances down her top on multiple occasions. Her feet were adorned with his sandals, which were also far too large. All this combined to make walking in the woods an unpleasant experience.

"How far are we from … anything?"

"There is a market two days' walk. Not far."

Robyn could still feel that same surging of power in her body. All her senses were heightened. She looked around the grove and the pool, the blanket Kivik had thrown around her, and the ancient trees surrounding the magic water. Robyn felt strong. Her arms and back contained a coursing river of energy, and her long legs felt coiled, ready to spring forward at a moment's call.

Her right heel dug into the hard earth as she looked down the forest path. Then, she began moving. Her legs started pumping fast. Robyn took off through the trees, their huge trunks whizzing by, leaves and branches snapping as she flew through them. The wood merely tickled her skin while ripping the clothes. The roar of the wind muffled Kivik's surprised shout as she vanished into the woods. She continued to run, feeling the surge of speed, power, and joy as she ran through the ancient forest. She could see so much so quickly. Her strong legs thumped in perfect rhythm. Slamming on the brakes, she halted like the Roadrunner, ready to go again in a second. Robyn took a quick turn and shot back down the lane.

Kivik's eyes were bulging when she returned. This goddess woman had barely broken a sweat. She ran as fast as Tullista in a full gallop. Her speed shocked the naturally stoic elf.

"I don't believe it," Robyn said quietly. "What's happened to me?"

"You've been blessed with a great gift. The spirits that live in this spring have imbued you with a special power. Please tell me how you've arrived here. I must know your tale."

"I don't know where to start. I was born on Earth, the third planet from the sun. Now I'm here. I took a swim, got a little frisky, and ended up with superpowers."

"What ritual did you perform to get such power?"

"I got crossfaded and fingered myself in the pool, then I saw you."

"You were quite strong with me—and forceful." Kivik's smile curled across his handsome face.

"I will be again." She reached down and grabbed his semi-hard cock. "But not yet.

"Yes, I think we both need a little recovery time."

"I'll be ready very soon—sooner than you." Robyn looked over the elf as if he were a piece of prime steak. "Better do some stretches, boy. Deep knee bends."

Kivik now had a full smile. "I'll be ready, my goddess, for anything."

"Good. You can start by removing your boots from my feet. They are far too big for my fine toes."

Kivik immediately bent to one knee and started taking off her boots. His hand on her thigh felt electric. His cock, now free of her firm grasp, called out for comfort, demanding a good firm grip. The elf began slowly stroking his cock.

"Not yet! Take that hand off that fine cock of yours! Get my damn boots off!"

Robyn loved this feeling of power and dominance over this powerful, blond Adonis, power over a warrior, power over a killer. Her cunny started dripping with each passing thought. How much control does she have? Where are his limits? What are hers? They had already started down a path, and they could not go back.

"My power demands pleasure, Kivik. I can feel it calling to me. It must be fed, and often, in all manner of ways. Are you able to deliver my pleasure, Kivik? Will you please your goddess?"

"I shall." Kivik looked up into his goddess's eyes. Two glowing rubies of light and color stared back at him. He knew he held no power to resist her demands. His only thoughts were focused on fulfilling his goddess's primal urges.

"In every way?" Robyn stood above the elf. She looked down on him, seeing Kivik in a veiled lavender haze. She could see his body temperature changing, increasing.

"In every way, my goddess."

"Take off the other boot."

Her left leg came up, and her foot rested on Kivik. The surge of power spiked slightly as she pressed the boot down onto his shoulder. "Take off the boot."

Elven hands moved quickly and smoothly to peel the calfskin leather from her supple stem. He ran his hands over her foot, admiring how smooth each toe felt, before moving up the leg, his hands massaging every inch of her ankle.

"I'm going to use your body for my demands."

"Yes, my goddess."

"You're going to be finished when I am done with you."

"Yes, my goddess."

Robyn took her foot off his shoulder. She stood in front of the elf with her hands on her hips. The winds caught her dark, wavy hair just perfectly enough to blow several strands across her strong features. "Remove your clothes," she commanded.

Kivik stood, his mind reeling. The words of this goddess in human form shot through his pointed ears and right to his cock. He knew what he must do. Once more, he ripped his jerkin over his broad shoulders and untied his breeches. As he pulled them over his ankles, his elven shaft stood straight and true. The elf cock bobbed in the afternoon sunlight.

Robyn had not yet seen it in full form; she'd only felt Kivik's shaft and controlled the cock like a puppet from inside the elf's ass. "Kivik, my pussy has been most satisfied today."

"Yes, goddess."

"But," Robyn paused, the yearning for more carnal pleasure welling up inside her, "my asshole is jealous—very jealous."

Kivik looked up at her with that same wry smile.

Robyn looked back, her eyes aflame. "So, I'm going to fuck yours to teach you a lesson on how to fuck mine." Her eyes were afire and unblinking as she looked at him.

Kivik's smile quickly fell.

"Now, go unsaddle that horse, and bring it here."

The elf hopped to his feet with another "yes, goddess." He walked slowly over to Tullista and unbuckled her saddle. Hefting the great weight of the war saddle onto his shoulder, he turned toward the still pool.

Robyn stood waiting. In her hands, she held a small jar, which she had discovered while rummaging through the handsome elf's equipment. She removed the stopper and plunged her index finger inside. The honey felt thick and gooey on her long finger. The gold color and texture felt good against her skin. Removing her finger, she gave it a long lick.

"I love honey. One of nature's greatest gifts. Don't you love honey, Kivik?"

"Yes, my goddess." He set the saddle down and turned back to face her.

"Good. You're going to get a lot of it." Her index finger plunged back into the jar, grabbing a great dollop of golden goodness. Upon removal, she placed her finger in front of Kivik's waiting mouth. "Open wide, boy." With that, her finger pushed into the elf.

His lips parted as the sweetened finger pulled out slightly and then pushed back in.

"Nice and slow. Suck every drop off me." She pulled away, and two fingers returned, both slathered in honey. They smeared across his mouth as she pushed deeper into him, his tongue swirling over her fingers.

His cock throbbed as he reached down to start to stroke himself.

Robyn pushed her hand into his mouth, gagging the elf. Grabbing the back of his strong neck with her free hand, she looked at him and spoke sternly. "I told you, no stroking. You will come when I'm finished with you. Not before, and not with your fucking hand. Do you understand?"

Kivik's mind reeled, needing release. He looked up into her eyes, her fingers in his mouth, as she locked her grip onto his neck. He simply nodded.

"Good boy." Robyn then put a third finger in his mouth. Her pussy ached with desire. Her asshole demanded a good hard fuck, but her heart and her mind wanted more. "Turn around."

Kivik began to stand.

"No, no. I said turn around." Her hard tone snapped him to attention. "Now!"

The elf, on his knees, shuffled 180 degrees, only to end up looking at his saddle. His property. His livelihood. The saddle that he used to ride into battle, to run down his enemies, and to drive collapsing armies from the field became his mattress. He knew the saddle would provide very little comfort for the punishment he was about to endure, yet if it pleased this commanding goddess, he would obey.

The voice in the back of Kivik's head screamed at him to run or fight, but the elven warrior ignored his fear, as he did before every battle, before every duel and match. The same voice that sized up the odds and told him things were hopeless quieted as a new voice could be heard in his head. *Obey your goddess. Provide your goddess with pleasure*

Kivik looked back over his shoulder at Robyn, his goddess. Her eyes were two blood rubies, glowing with a terrible and dark passion. Robyn stood before her broken submissive, still clothed in his breeches and shirt, staring at his bare, exposed, and vulnerable ass.

"Get over the saddle boy. Take your place before me."

Robyn had never felt such a throbbing call from her own body. The world around her swirled in colors she could not define, her ears heard scents from flowers, and she could smell her very energy. Robyn had come five times since she entered the pool, and the effects were far from wearing off; in fact, they were building within her, growing stronger, demanding more from her and of Kivik. Robyn couldn't make sense of the feelings rushing across her full breasts, twisting through her hardened nipples, shooting down her stomach, and churning in her pussy and ass. She would have this warrior, she would break him, and then she would let him have her, in all ways.

All of Kivik's attention suddenly focused on his open ass. A warm, gooey sensation began to slowly creep down the crack of his ass. The honey stopped and pooled in his bung, before beginning the slow, inevitable trickle inside.

"You're lucky you're an elf—no body hair. This stuff is a bitch to get out," Robyn whispered into his pointed, trembling ear as she pushed her left index finger slowly into his waiting ass.

Robyn's pulsating eyes. His smile moved slowly across his face before breaking into a broad grin. "Yes, goddess."

His strength began to fill him with a terrible desire, and with that desire came a new focus. *Fuck this goddess in the ass until she comes, and when she does come, fill her asshole with your seed. Please your goddess. Give her pleasure.*

Robyn bent her thick, round ass over the saddle faster than a jackrabbit on a date. Her new toy had earned her rear, and she wanted to give him a treat for being such a good bottom. The saddle felt slick with sweat, shame, and lust. Kivik's hands were on her, ripping down her breeches, leaving her bare asshole exposed for the world, whatever world this may be. Her asshole and pussy were out and open. She could feel the wet pressure, not of honey, but of a long tongue beginning to lick and tickle her tight, horny bung.

The raw aroma of this goddess's cunny and pussy filled Kivik's mind and body. He loved to lick and eat ass and pussy, but this hole tasted the most divine. His long tongue snaked out and began to swirl around Robyn's round and ready asshole.

"Yeah, boy, get in there and lick it clean."

The elf's tongue swirled, poked, and probed deeper into her tasty, wet bung. The flavor of copper and nutmeg only drove him to lick harder and faster against her smooth, rubbery hole and pliable bung. Each lick probed deeper and deeper into her most forbidden area. Saliva dripped down as Kivik lapped up her pussy juice, swished it in his mouth, and spit it into her asshole, lubing her ass for the fuck to come. His strong hands pressed against her pussy lips, rubbing them in a slow circle.

"Don't touch my pussy. I don't want to be aware of my pussy. You just focus on my asshole, like a good little licking slut. Lick my ass, get it wet, and lick my ass with your whole tongue! Harder!"

Kivik began to extend his tongue. It pushed deeper and deeper into her yielding hole, moving three, four, then five inches deep. The muscle moved and pushed with a mind all its own, tickling and touching all the secret places in her ass all at once.

"That's it. Fuck my ass with your tongue. Get up in there and lick my dirty asshole."

Now it was Robyn's turn to start spinning. Her mind began to race with furious abandon. This amazing tongue stoked her inner fire, building her passion higher than ever before. "Fuck my asshole! Please fuck my asshole, Kivik! Fuck me hard. Fuck me until I come! Just fuck me!"

Wordlessly, the tongue slowly wriggled out of her throbbing bung. Her ass needed to be filled. She needed to get fucked, get used, and watch this adonis fill her ass with his cum.

Kivik's cock stood like a bowsprit. Hard and strong, it pointed the way to glory and pleasure. Robyn's asshole was a beacon for the elf's cock to focus on. He slowly stroked his cock, making it grow larger and harder than before. The elf pressed his blessed meat against the yielding flesh of the human's bung.

Robyn could feel the pressure of Kivik's thick, hard shaft. She reached back with both hands and pulled her cheeks apart, opening her ass for him further. "This is your ass now, boy, and you better fuck this ass hard. Your goddess needs to come." Her eyes were fire.

Kivik entered Robyn's ass with a slow and steady push. *Please your goddess. Fill her with pleasure.* The command shot through his head again. Kivik began to thrust his shaft into his goddess's ass.

"Good boy," Robyn grunted. "Fuck my hole. Fuck my hole like I fucked yours!"

Kivik began to thrust harder and faster. He could feel the bottom of her ass and pushed in further. As he did, the human let out another groaning grunt.

She pushed back, her ass swallowing his cock. "Harder! Fuck me!"

Kivik could feel his cock begin to swell even further. His thickening shaft pushed her anal walls to their limit.

It was Robyn's mind balancing pleasure, desire, and shame now. The feeling of this otherworldly, ever-growing cock filling her ass canal was becoming more than she could comprehend. Kivik's thrusts banged into the deepest recesses of her soul.

Kivik's cock began its march toward orgasm. The shaft began to buzz slightly, slowly growing in intensity.

"Fucking magic dick!" Robyn shouted as her orgasm burst loose from deep inside her ass. The orgasm exploded out of her, originating from deep in her backside and radiating out through her pussy, hips, stomach, and breasts. Deep, otherworldly moans, grunts, and screams filled the quiet forest grove as Robyn's ass spasmed and came again and again to Kivik's vibrating cock.

With each deep and rough thrust, Kivik drew closer and closer to his desired orgasm. Robyn's assquake pushed his over the edge. The vibrations in his shaft reached a fevered pitch as he bore down on the human goddess, her ass in the air, and filled her with his meat. His body was shaking from the inside out. His cock was growing and pushing her walls out beyond the limits of pain and pleasure as he came.

Robyn felt the orgasm approaching and pushed her ass up and his cock even deeper into her. The spasming of Kivik's engorged and spurting cock set off another string of deep tissue rockets within her body. She could feel the elf come in her hot and stretched ass.

The two lovers lay together in stunned silence for what seemed like an eternity. The pair entwined around each other in a sticky, fucked, and silly pile. Robyn, a full and towering six feet, taller now than when she started the day, stood first. The power and energy of the spring and the fuck grew stronger inside of her.

Needing a rinse, Robyn slowly walked toward the pool. She waded into the pond, the water lapping and licking at her. The tingle from before still existed, yet this time it was different, darker. Splashing water onto her face, she took a quick dive. The water again surrounded her with millions of tingling kisses and pulses.

When her head broke the surface again, she walked slowly back to shore, her tall, powerful frame glistening with water droplets in the dappled sunlight of the forest. Kivik was asleep, exhausted from the fervent rutting he had just experienced. Robyn looked down on the gorgeous elf, his blond mane pooled around him, and noticed his magic dick, still impressive while limp and spent.

She noticed something else as well. There was a red mark on her body that had not been there before. Two crimson triangles met at their points just below her navel, making what looked like an hourglass. "Must be from the saddle," she muttered, rubbing her stomach.

As her fingers touched the hourglass, a new urge began to fill her body. A darker, needier hunger rose from within her body and mind. Robyn moved without thinking, acting on a deep and long-dormant instinct. The hourglass turned from a shade of crimson to a vibrant scarlet. She stood over the recumbent elven warrior, gently placing her hands on his delicate, angled features. She could feel the elf's energy through her fingers as she held his face. Robyn leaned into Kivik and kissed him gently on the lips.

Kivik responded slowly, awoken by this warm embrace. His deep-blue eyes met hers for one last time and then widened as he looked into the fire of her. Robyn held the First Spear firmly in place as she kissed Kivik, drawing his essence out of the shocked and dying elf. Robyn drew pure light and energy from the warrior; his essence, identity, soul, and spirit left his body and filled hers, satisfying her hunger. Kivik made no sound. He couldn't struggle, and he fought no final glorious battle.

When Robyn released the corpse of her lover, it fell to the ground in a cloud of dust, leaving only the skull in her hand. She stared at what had been her lover's perfect face without a word, without an exclamation. Robyn Tanhill, former secretary, former call center employee, dropped the skull and watched it splinter into shards and powder.

Changes in her had begun. She knew that she now bore powers of speed, strength, and sexual energy beyond her wildest dreams and that this power must be fed. She stood taller, could run faster than a deer, possessed great strength, and could outfuck anybody who questioned her. This wonderful power must be fed by souls. Robyn knew this intrinsically. She felt these changes filling her body. Instinct told her to steal Kivik's soul, and she felt no remorse or guilt. Only one emotion truly scared her; she enjoyed the entire experience.

"Goodbye, Kivik. Thanks for the magic dick, and sorry you're now compost. Your soul tasted like figs and golden raspberries, so well done. You have served your new goddess well."

With that, she donned the elf's breeches with their silver filigree and the leather doublet depicting a dozen battles. Wrapping the belt and dagger around her waist, she discovered a leather drawstring purse filled with peppercorns and three copper coins. The boots, she tossed; they were far too large, and she didn't need them anyway.

Finally, she looked at Tullista, the great warhorse, who was tied to a nearby oak. "It's your lucky day, horse." Quick as a flash, the bridle fell from the beast's head, and the reigns were tossed aside. Robyn slapped Tullista on her brown rump and sent her running. The horse didn't need prompting and tore down the eastern forest path at breakneck pace, thumping and whinnying until out of earshot. Robyn watched the great horse run, tempted to give chase, but thought better of herself. Her new hunger had been sated by the soul and essence of Kivik of Muren, First Spear of the Line.

Robyn turned west, away from the fleeing horse, and away from her spring. She turned away from the pile of Kivik dust and toward the road. She plucked the silver spear from the ground, still filthy and sticky from her recent fuck, and simply walked away.

"Time to see what this new world has to offer," Robyn said aloud. "Time for this goddess to stretch her wings."

Contributors

H.R. Hypolita

HR Hypolita lives and works as a writer of erotic fantasy and fiction in Portland Oregon. When not delving deep into sexual fantasy and horror Hypolita enjoys the outdoors of the Pacific Northwest.

January Wren

January Wren is a romance author and dabbles in the horror genre too (though you won't find her sleeping in the dark!). She is an undergraduate student, one that can usually be found with a cat on her lap, and an iced coffee in her hand. She currently resides on the east coast and is glad that writing doesn't require her to be outside, covered in three feet of snow from December through April!

You can read her fanfiction on Archive of Our Own or connect with her via Tumblr (@Januarywren).

Max Carrey

Max Carrey currently lives in sunny California. She loves delving into her characters complicated pasts and suspense filled futures.

She's had stories appear in Zimbell House's *The Dead Game* and *Spirit Walker*. Chipper Press' *The Princess*. As well as upcoming releases with PCC Inscape Magazine and Impulsive Walrus.

To stay up to date follow her at:
instagram.com/maxcarrey/

Shanjida Nusrath Ali

Shanjida is an Indie author hat first started writing on Wattpad. Then with the love and support of her readers, she self-published her first eBook series, *Destroyed* (Dark Love Due#1) and *Freed* (Dark Love Due#2).

Meanwhile, when she isn't writing, Shanjida spends her free time reading books or improving her art skills as she also is an Art student. Living in Bangladesh with her family and completing her studies in English Language and Art.

Wolfgang Domino

Wolfgang Domino is passionate about writing erotica. He lives in the woods of Maine, enjoys chess, cycling and reading. Some of his work has appeared on Myerotica.com and Literotica.com.

Wolfgang is currently working on a novella he hopes to finish sometime next year.

Other Works from Temptation Press

Summer Fling

Kiss & Tell

The Professor

Private Lessons

Choices

This Sub's for You

Intimate Moments

Forbidden

The Boss

Nights in the City

The Match Game

Royal Pr9otection

How to Thank a Contributor

Dear Reader,

Everyone at Temptation Press would like to thank you for reading *Marked: An Erotic Collection*. If you would like to thank a particular contributor, the best way is to leave a review for them. You may do so by leaving one on our Goodreads page, under the title, *Marked*, by using the link below:

http://www.goodreads.com/TemptationPress

and be sure to mention the contributor directly.

Why should you leave a review? Reviews help budding authors build their credibility in the book industry. By posting a review on Goodreads and other review sites, you help other readers find new authors they may wish to follow, and you never know, your review may end up on an author's website one day.

Friend us on Goodreads:
https://www.goodreads.com/TemptationPress

Visit our website:
http://www.TemptationPress.com